THE LEGACY SERIES

SERIES TITLES

American Animism
Jamey Gallagher

Keeping What's Best Left Kept Secret
David Ricchiute

Soaked
Toby LeBlanc

The Path of Totality
Marie Zhuikov

Shocker in Gloomtown
Dan Libman

The Continental Divide
Bob Johnson

The Three Devils and Other Stories
William Luvaas

The Correct Response
Manfred Gabriel

Welcome Back to the World: A Novella & Stories
Rob Davidson

Greyhound Cowboy and Other Stories
Ken Post

Close Call
Kim Suhr

The Waterman
Gary Schanbacher

Signs of the Imminent Apocalypse and Other Stories
Heidi Bell

What We Might Become
Sara Reish Desmond

The Silver State Stories
Michael Darcher

An Instinct for Movement
Michael Mattes

The Machine We Trust
Tim Conrad

Gridlock
Brett Biebel

Salt Folk
Ryan Habermeyer

The Commission of Inquiry
Patrick Nevins

Maximum Speed
Kevin Clouther

Reach Her in This Light
Jane Curtis

The Spirit in My Shoes
John Michael Cummings

*The Effects of Urban Renewal on Mid-Century America and
Other Crime Stories*
Jeff Esterholm

What Makes You Think You're Supposed to Feel Better
Jody Hobbs Hesler

Fugitive Daydreams
Leah McCormack

Hoist House: A Novella & Stories
Jenny Robertson

Finding the Bones: Stories & A Novella
Nikki Kallio

Self-Defense
Corey Mertes

Where Are Your People From?
James B. De Monte

Sometimes Creek
Steve Fox

The Plagues
Joe Baumann

The Clayfields
Elise Gregory

Kind of Blue
Christopher Chambers

Evangelina Everyday
Dawn Burns

Township
Jamie Lyn Smith

Responsible Adults
Patricia Ann McNair

Great Escapes from Detroit
Joseph O'Malley

Nothing to Lose
Kim Suhr

The Appointed Hour
Susanne Davis

Jamey Gallagher is a master of simple, poignant narratives of displacement, dislocation, and abandonment. The stress here—as it should be—is on the emotional lives, the quiet inner storms, of individuals enduring or recovering from dramas and traumas. No specific location, apart from North America itself, limits Gallagher's vision and concern, and as a whole these sad sojourns and whispery odysseys produce a detailed topography of the bumpy swales of the American soul. A brilliant debut.

—J.C. HALLMAN
author of *Say Anarcha*

Damn, these stories are good. The lean prose recalls the best of noir fiction, but there's more here than first meets the eye. Unflinching forays into such a dizzying array of worlds, narrators, and dramatic situations that it's hard to believe they all came from the same imagination. You can't predict where these stories are going, but you quickly realize it will be worth the ride. Buckle up and hang on.

—CHRISTOPHER CHAMBERS
author of *Kind of Blue*

AMERICAN ANIMISM

STORIES

JAMEY GALLAGHER

CORNERSTONE PRESS
UNIVERSITY OF WISCONSIN-STEVENS POINT

Cornerstone Press, Stevens Point, Wisconsin 54481
Copyright © 2025 Jamey Gallagher
www.uwsp.edu/cornerstone

Printed in the United States of America by
Point Print and Design Studio, Stevens Point, Wisconsin

Library of Congress Control Number: 2025932051
ISBN: 978-1-960329-71-4

Cover art by Evangeline Gallagher.

Cornerstone Press titles are produced in courses and internships offered by the
Department of English at the University of Wisconsin–Stevens Point.

DIRECTOR & PUBLISHER
Dr. Ross K. Tangedal

EXECUTIVE EDITORS
Jeff Snowbarger, Freesia McKee

EDITORIAL DIRECTOR
Brett Hill

SENIOR EDITOR
Ellie Atkinson

PRESS STAFF
Cora Bender, Lillian Kulbeck, Kylie Newton, Sophie McPherson, Madison Schultz,
Ava Willett

For Kris Messer. You blow me away.

STORIES

Monster Girl Survives Close Call

She returned to work at the cryptid museum a week after the attack. She still felt a little unsteady, her brain half submerged in weird murk, but she refused to let it show. She was Monster Girl, and Monster Girl showed no weakness. Really she was D, but she thought of herself as Monster Girl, at least sometimes. She wore black t-shirts, jeans, and Chuck Taylors, and she didn't care what anyone thought of her.

"What up, D?" Hal said. Hal had no idea what happened to her, only that she'd taken a week off. She doubted he'd even asked why. He was that incurious. Hal was fifteen years older than her, but they shared the same interests: *Attack on Titan*, Junji Ito, black metal, science, and, of course, cryptids and the paranormal. They got along well. Like siblings—the kind who were close, not like D and her actual sister, who hated each other. She and Hal teased each other mercilessly, digging into their most tender spots with a cruel kind of love. She wasn't sure Hal had ever had a girlfriend, and sometimes that made her sad, but his love life sure wasn't her responsibility. Very early on she'd made it clear that he had no chance with her, and after a few tentative sniffings around her he'd given up on anything more than friendship. She didn't want to know what he thought about her or what he imagined when he was away from the museum. That was his business.

"Not much, Big Hal. You been holding it down since I've been gone?"

"Nonstop action. It's good to have you back." For a second she thought he might be sincere.

The morning passed like almost every other morning at the cryptid museum. They traded off giving tours and working the register. People would wander into the space, built inside half of an old hangar not far off the Parkway, on a long road between the Pine Barrens and the Jersey Shore, and gather in the lobby, looking around them at the six life-sized figures of cryptids edging the oval room: Mothman, Bigfoot, Wendigo, Chupacabra, Yeti, and, of course, in the place of honor, their very own local legend, the Jersey Devil. When there were enough of them—typically seven or eight—the next tour would embark, wending its way through the space. It was a cool museum featuring relatively realistic scenery made by a prop designer out of Atlantic City. There were four environments: pine barren, mountain forest, desert, and rainforest. The soundtrack was ambient, piped in through hidden speakers. There were actual artifacts—a supposed mummy, a faked mermaid, a real walrus penis. Videos of witnesses, almost all men, with wild eyes, in rural settings, played on big old televisions in the corners, the volume set low. They talked about their encounters with this or that monster. D loved it all and still remembered the first time she'd come to the museum, as a visitor, with a boyfriend-of-the-moment, a very short-lived relationship. The dude had scoffed through the first two rooms until she told him to get the fuck away from her so she could experience the museum the way she wanted to: as a freefall into faith.

She'd noticed the Help Wanted sign by the register that first time, hadn't believed her luck when she got the job on the spot.

It was not exactly a stepping stone to anything else, the pay was minimum wage, and the hours sucked, yet… it was a job she loved, and how many people could say that about their jobs? A precious few.

Sometimes Bob Sacchis, the owner of the museum, would make his way through the lobby on some harried research mission. He would hurry up to the "library" on the loft floor of the museum, above the rainforest, and flip through one of the books for a while, as if on the verge of discovering something new or something forgotten, his eyebrows creased. At first D had taken it all for show. Sacchis had wild white hair and a double chin, and he played the part of the mad cryptozool-ogist perfectly, but then she realized (she thought; she was pretty sure) that he was sincere. Now she wondered if even *he* knew where the performance ended and the authenticity began. She knew for sure that Sacchis believed he'd had an up-and-close encounter with the Jersey Devil, back in the heady days of the 1970s. He'd been camping alone in the Pine Barrens, on some kind of visionquest, when the beast appeared at dusk, outlined on his tent wall, pressing against the canvas, breathing its rancid breath. It smelled like it'd been eating voles and snakes, Sacchis claimed. A hot, hoary breath. Later, when the beast was apparently gone, he ventured out of the tent to search for footprints or spoor. The last thing he remembered, before coming to, on a rock down by a river in the barrens a mile and a half from his camp, was a shadow approaching, blotting out the night sky.

At first D thought Sacchis was full of shit—or delu-sional, one or the other. Now, though, she could relate. Not to the Jersey Devil part of the story, but to waking up some-where, all memory gone. Having to piece it all back together. Being left with a piece missing. The pull of unsolvable and personal mystery.

She and Hal had a healthy sibling-esque rivalry, con-stantly bickering over who could give the best tour. Hal claimed people only liked her because she was young and cute (overstatements on both counts, in her opinion), but

Hal could hold his own. He had a certain dramatic flair, thanks to a couple years of high school drama and his participation in some local productions—*Pippin*, the *Technicolor Dreamcoat*. They were both good at holding the interest even of the skeptics, and the customers were split about evenly into thirds between those who were apathetic on the subject of the paranormal in general and cryptids in particular, those who were Believers, and those who were Doubters/Debunkers/Skeptics. The latter were the worst. They were killjoys and elitists. They reminded D of the boy who'd taken her to the museum that first time. They thought they were better than everyone else, could see through the bullshit other people fell for, when really they were just superior fucks. Anyone who didn't take mystery seriously was a fool, in her humble opinion.

After lunch, attendance slowed, and she and Hal hung out like a couple buds, showing each other videos and memes on their phones, talking about new releases, listening to Norwegian black metal over the stereo system in the lobby/gift shop. While recovering from the attack, D had reread all of Junji Ito, gaining even more respect for the revered graphic novelist. His work, almost all horror aside from his cat diaries, was unsurpassed. It still creeped her out, filled her dreams with images of men transforming into snails and robots covered with rotting flesh, pustulence and darkness, but also… love. As cheesy as it sounded, sometimes reading Ito made D feel the strong desire to be in a relationship. God help her.

Around three o'clock, a couple entered the museum. The man was nearly a foot shorter than the woman but unusually handsome, with bright teeth and a nice smile, his dark hair shaved close to the scalp on the sides, longer and slicked back on top. He was perfect, aside from the fact that it looked like someone had cracked him across the nose with a lead pipe. His nose was bifurcated down the middle, giving him the look of an old-school pugilist. The woman had long blonde hair and wore a tan trenchcoat, and D could tell she was older than the man because of the tendons on her neck. Visitors from Atlantic City, no doubt.

They bought tour tickets from Hal, who told them they would wait a few minutes to see if anyone else showed up. While waiting, the couple wandered around looking at the t-shirts and books in the gift shop, the figures of the cryptids arranged around the edge of the oval room. It was impossible for D to get a read on the couple. They could have been Believers, Skeptics, or Apathetics. Usually she could tell right away, but not with them. The couple ushered in a chill with them, as if they'd just finished, or were in the middle of, a serious fight. D closed her eyes and felt herself swaying, her brain swimming in a thick soup. She'd been okay throughout the morning, but now she wondered if she hadn't pushed herself too hard. She was still recuperating. She should have been lying down.

She pulled out all the stops for the couple's tour, trying to emote and be mysterious, but got almost nothing back from them, and she felt like a little chirpy bird. They looked at her, the smile on the man's face transforming slowly into a smirk. She felt like what she imagined a new teacher would feel in front of an unresponsive class, and after a while she slid into the script and stopped trying so hard.

The couple spent a lot of time in the rainforest. They looked at the recreation of the world's largest snake, an anaconda as thick as a redwood. The man stood in a corner of the room watching a couple locals from Oaxaca talk about their experience with the Chupacabra on the TV while the woman wandered around as if she were in an actual rainforest, touching the leaves with her fingers, running her hand over the snakeskin, her heels clicking metronomically on the tile floor.

While they wandered, D mentally flashed on the man who attacked her. The incident had been coming back to her this way all week, in sudden unstoppable flickers.

She'd been waiting for her friend Mel at the Hard Rock Cafe on Saturday night. They were going to hit the casinos, have a night of drinking and talking and laughing, the way they had once before. Mel was a girl she'd met at the community college, where she'd taken a few classes in a converted convention center. They met in their math class and bonded over a mutual love of Japanese culture. Mel was into more mainstream anime, not the horror stuff D was into, but, still, she was the best friend D had had in years. She had great hope for them. Both were General Studies majors, and neither had any real idea what they wanted to do with their lives, though D was learning toward Biology. She imagined a future D in the field studying the dwindling number of species during the Sixth Extinction.

"Going to be late. Order some food," Mel texted, then, thirty minutes later, when D was digging into a burger done medium rare, blood pooling on the white plate, a Poison song blasting over the restaurant's sound system, she texted, "Sorry. Can't make it." No explanation. Not even a frowning emoji. D shrugged off her annoyance—the least she deserved was some kind of explanation—finished the burger, then went to the bar and ordered a margarita that came in what looked like a gallon glass and drank. The music was horrible, but a fun kind of horrible, mostly hair metal from the 80s. Whitesnake, Skid Row. Mötley Crüe. The best it got was Dio. She watched the bartenders, who moved with a kind of rough hipster ease. The man had tattoos and spiked hair; the woman showed cleavage without looking slutty. She had hair like Amy Winehouse and tattoos on her clavicle. D tried not to feel jealous, but everyone around her seemed like they were with someone else, and everyone seemed happy and at ease. Partying it up.

She left the bar half-drunk and walked toward the end of the boardwalk to see the ocean away from the crowds. The rolling chairs on the boardwalk had always made her uncomfortable. Atlantic City had stated as a resort for convalescents, and the rolling chairs were throwbacks to the wheelchairs used by invalids, but now the people who rode in them were mealy-faced tourists who just wanted to have someone pushing them, someone they could boss around. Some sick fantasy of class mobility.

She heard the footsteps before she came to the edge of the populated part of the boardwalk, but at first she ignored them, refusing to give in to paranoia. She knew she was prone to it. The margarita helped ward off her anxiety. And why would someone be following her anyway? Who was she? Just some girl on a Saturday night. She turned casually to see the man behind her. They were almost alone, on the edge of the lights. In the half-light, the man seemed almost handsome. His broad shoulders tapered down to a narrow waist. Something about him reminded her of Sonic the Hedgehog. His eyes, maybe, or his spiky hair. It was absurd, but she couldn't shake the connection. She was being followed by Sonic the Hedgehog. His eyes lit up when he noticed her looking back, and there was no question about it: he was not only following her, not only pursuing her; he was hunting her.

She didn't waste time. She ran, her Chucks finding purchase on the boardwalk. She wondered now why she hadn't turned around and made her way past him, back toward the light, toward people, civilization, safety. Instead, she ran toward the darkness of the beach and the ocean, as if there was ever safety in shadows, his footsteps pounding hard behind her. When she tripped on the stairs leading to the beach, he was on her. She wanted to cry out but had no time. She felt something heavy hit her head and then…

She shook herself out of the memory and led the couple into the last room, the one that looped back to the lobby/gift shop, where another version of the Jersey Devil was posed, its wings raised dramatically behind it. Its face looked realistic, teeth and jowls and wild eyes rendered perfectly. The set designer had done an impressive job, and even after she'd seen it a thousand or more times this Devil had still made her uneasy. Until now. Now it had no effect. Whatever.

The couple stood under the beast, smirking.

"Take our picture." The man handed D his phone. He was used to giving orders and having them obeyed. For the first time, the woman removed her sunglasses, revealing eyes that looked smaller and more vulnerable than D had imagined. Somehow that made her more attractive. Stunning, really, like an old school movie star, Jean Harlow or something. D lined up the shot. His hand was splayed across her shoulder. Their perfect faces. He looked kind of stupid, a foot shorter than her. Fuck you, she thought as she snapped the pictures.

They bought two t-shirts, a Jersey Devil for him, a Chupacabra for her, and left. No tip.

"You win some you lose some," Hal said.

"Ain't that the truth."

Around five they started cleaning—there was nothing much to clean, but it was the routine. D dreaded leaving for the day, didn't want to go back to her apartment, but felt the need for a nap. She was so tired. All she really wanted to do was take a shower, slip into some sweatpants, watch TV, eat popcorn, and fall asleep with her cat on her lap. She wanted to empty herself out.

"Hey," Hal said as he counted down the drawer, and she worried, because he sounded the way he had when he'd been trying to see if he had any shot with her, skittish, "I got something to tell you."

"Well, tell me, asshole. Don't draw it out."

"I gave my two weeks'…"

"Wait, what?"

"Yeah. I'm moving. To Phoenix. Ha. Can you believe that? Me in Phoenix."

"No," she said, because she couldn't. Hal in Phoenix? Uh, no. "Whyy?" She could hear the whine in her voice. It didn't sound like her at all.

He shrugged. "Opportunity knocks."

She'd forgotten Hal had a degree in Geology, that he'd been looking for jobs in his field since she first met him. She'd forgotten he existed outside this place. She couldn't picture him as anything other than Hal from the Pine Barren Cryptid Museum.

"We should get a drink. Celebrate or something. Not tonight, though," she said.

"You know it."

D felt a strange urge to hug him, this weird man who was closer to her than her own sister, but she didn't. They said goodnight the way they always did, from a distance. Then she drove home and did exactly what she'd wanted to. By eight o'clock she was asleep with the cat on her hip. By two a.m. she was awake again, crawling out of a dream that was like a memory of the attack and the attacker.

She came to on the beach, with a rock by her side, the rock that must have hit her head. Her head was bruised, but her skull was not broken. A contusion. She staggered to the urgent care center, where they told her she had a concussion. She told them she'd hit her head on a rock after falling on the beach—she wasn't sure why. Maybe because she didn't want to have to deal with cops and police reports. Didn't want to admit the attack had happened.

In her dream the attacker slobbered over her, his teeth dripping ooze, his hands strong on her skull then on her neck as he choked her. The motherfucker.

She scrolled on her phone since she knew she would not be sleeping again.

She knew she'd been lucky to survive the attack but not how lucky until she saw an article linked to a tweet about a spate of murders in Atlantic City over the past three months. The victims were all young women. In the photos that accompanied the article, she saw herself. All the victims were about her age, all dark-haired, all much less lucky than she was because they were all dead, their bodies found mutilated and naked in dark pockets of the city. A cold shiver ran through her. She imagined someone must have approached from the boardwalk to stop him from doing what he wanted to do with her, someone or something must have scared him off. She'd been a fraction away from a very different, far more traumatic experience.

In the shower at three a.m., she couldn't help but look down at her body and imagine it not her own but as something dead and discarded, thrown away.

She sat curled on her easy chair in the front room, drinking coffee, staring at the walls.

She'd never been so happy to get back to the cryptid museum. There was a heightened quality to the day, less busy than the day before, since they both knew their days together were numbered. They still ragged on each other, but there was a different quality to the ragging, a kind of sad sweetness to it. Sometimes she wanted to punch Hal. How could he leave her here all alone? Sometimes she wanted to hug him. He was venturing out to pursue his own life, and a life in Phoenix as a geologist *had* to be better than a life as a tour guide at a cryptid museum in South Jersey. Didn't it?

She got the idea when Bob Sacchis made his way through the lobby yet again. Instead of going to the library upstairs, Sacchis wended his way to the pine barren room and watched the video of the witnesses who'd seen the Jersey Devil. He scratched something into a little notepad he carried with him, looking like he'd forgotten something essential to his life on earth.

"I have a better idea than getting a drink, Big Hal."

"Oh yeah? What's that?"

"A tracking expedition." She gestured toward Sacchis.

"Are you serious?"

"As a heart attack."

Sacchis was only too eager to help them plan the expedition, taking out maps he'd been annotating ever since his sighting, telling them where he thought the den of the Devil might be, showing them where he'd camped, where he'd come to near the river. She hadn't seen Sacchis so animated since starting at the museum. He was so excited she asked him to join them, but, fortunately, he declined, shaking his head.

"It's up to you two now," he said, passing the torch to them.

Hal showed up outside her apartment that morning wearing a safari hat and a black Rob Zombie t-shirt. His calves below the khaki shorts were pale and thin. She wondered if this was the stupidest idea she'd ever had. She would now have to spend two whole days with this man she barely knew. She trusted him, but still.

She threw her tent and backpack into the back of his Cube, and they drove to the food store. Hal had cookware, so they bought steak and potatoes, aluminum foil, a six-pack of lime White Claws, and snacks. They parked by a trailhead and ventured in. It was funny, using an actual map when they both had smartphones, but they used the map exclusively. Hal was fixated on it, following the line Sacchis had made with his finger, looking around, nodding once in a while.

The hiking was cake—the Pine Barrens were basically flat for hundreds of miles around, aside from a few rivers and caves, a cranberry bog here and there—and buggy. After a while they settled into a steady rhythm. They talked about the last season of *Attack on Titan*, comparing notes, more or less agreeing on every plot point.

Everything was fine until they got to the campsite where Sacchis had set up his stuff those many years ago. Someone had camped there recently. There were half-burnt logs, plus old pages scattered here and there. She didn't realize they were porn at first. They bagged them and said nothing. Went off separately to fetch firewood, set up their tents. By the time everything was done there were hours to go before nightfall. She felt it again, that lopsided feeling in her brain. She wondered if the attack had done permanent damage. She felt… dark and sad. Like most teenagers, D had suffered from depression, but mostly it had just been this. Dark moods.

"Taking a nap," she said, heading into her tent.

Hal nodded. He'd set up a camp chair and was reading a comic book. She settled into her sleeping bag and thought bad thoughts, dark thoughts. What the hell was she doing here?

At about five, a text from Mel woke her. It was a long text, and she was worried at first, but then she realized it was a confession: Mel was telling her that she'd stood her up the other night because she had real feelings for her, and was scared of those feelings. It was kind of sweet. The girl had a crush on her. She thought about Mel. She hadn't considered her in that light, but now that she did.… She hated to leave her on read, but she would have to think carefully about how to respond.

Hal had made the fire and settled the cookstove over it.

"Maybe the smell of blood will entice the Devil out of his hiding place," he said. He lifted the raw steak next to his face and smiled. Blood dripped onto the fire and crackled. She smiled at him and dipped into the snacks, opening a White Claw.

It was a pleasant night, in every way. They ate—the food was delicious—talked and laughed. Hal was funny. He was exactly the same outside of the museum as he was inside, a real mensch. She could tell he'd had a rough adolescence. In her opinion, all the best people had.

"I'm going to miss you, Hal," she said. His face was lit by the fire, changing, changing.

"I'm going to miss you, too," he said. A rare moment of sincerity. It passed.

Sometime after midnight they went out hunting the Jersey Devil. The beast was supposed to be nocturnal. They sure as hell weren't going to sneak up on him, because they were loud, and the light from her cellphone and the beam of his flashlight lit everything up. Shadows crawled and ran. They stopped often to listen, not expecting to hear anything.

She knew she should go to the police and give them a description of the man who'd attacked her—Sonic the fucking Hedgehog, with his wild eyes and spiked hair. She should have done it that night, and she sure as hell should have done it after reading the article about the spate of attacks, murders, rapes. She had no excuse for waiting. He could have been out there right now, somewhere near the edge of the lights in Atlantic City, waiting for another poor woman to wander away from safety. She could stop him.

They found a cave, but it was not deep and there was nothing inside. They saw nothing but trees and more trees, could spot no tracks in the darkness, so they wandered back to the campsite.

She was buzzed but not drunk, and it was almost two a.m. by the time they got into their separate tents. It was strange the way tents could make things sound closer. Hal was at least ten feet away, yet it felt like he was right next to her, getting out of his shorts, putting on soft pants, breathing in the darkness. Her head was lined up by his feet. It was strange to be together like this, intimate but not intimate at all. It was too warm and humid, and D felt herself sweating.

"Did you hear that?" Hal called over a few minutes later.

"No."

A long stretch of silence. Maybe an owl in the night.

"I'm scared," Hal said.

"You should be. I hear he has a taste for middle aged men."

"Fuck you. Not that."

"I know," she said. Hal was scared of going to Phoenix and starting a new life. Scared of being alone. Scared of never finding anyone. He deserved someone, though she couldn't imagine who would be right for him.

"It's scary," she said.

"I don't know if I'm really going to go."

"Of course you're going to go, you moron," she said. He didn't respond again. Maybe he was sleeping already.

She was Monster Girl, she reminded herself. She was strong. She half-slept, coming to to listen to creatures rustling through the pines. There were definitely deer out here. There was plenty of prey for the Devil to feast on.

In the morning they hiked down to the river where Sacchis had come to after his attack. They both imagined him, almost fifty years earlier, with his long hair and his mustache. A young man on some kind of quest to find himself. Maybe he had, D thought. Maybe he'd found himself the night the Jersey Devil came and took him away into the Pine Barrens. Maybe he was lucky.

She looked at Hal, who stared into the water. He wore the Rob Zombie shirt and the safari hat and his skin looked slicked with sweat. She could smell him from where she stood, an almost unpleasant odor that did not make her look forward to the ride back.

"That was wild last night," he said. "The wings. You saw its wings, right?" His eyes moved across the river, refusing to look up at her. "You saw it? Right?"

She looked into the river—it was really just a creek—then into the endless expanse of tree trunks. She tried to imagine a creature that would *choose* to live here, hiding away from humankind. She could kind of get it.

"Sure I did," she said.

If I Ran My Hand Over Your Head, I Would Bleed

It was the purest of incidental contacts, not even contact really since we didn't touch skin to skin but skin to jacket sleeve, a wool suit jacket sleeve against my hairless arm, shaved for the purpose of hydrodynamics, which immediately set the pattern for our strange intertwining gender positions, her with her suit jacket, hair cut so short you could see her scalp on the sides, a pierced eyebrow and earlobes, eyes accentuated by eyeliner, dramatic, almost Egyptian, while I wore a sleeveless t-shirt and my running tights, package kept securely in place by molded codpiece undershorts, my sleek bright yellow running sneakers, my stubbled face, which had not been shaved since six a.m. the day before and here it was nine a.m. We had jostled against each other outside the airport, which she had just flown into and which I had just run to, because it was a good run and I liked to watch people enter the Southwest, dazed from hours of air travel, some awed by the starkness of the all-brown landscape, the hot dry sun. I liked to let sweat cool while I wandered around baggage claim, which you can get to without passing through security, hands on my hips, looking at the people lining up to rent rental cars or get a shuttle bus ticket to Santa Fe, the anxious waiting for the carousel to click into action, the occasional shuffling airline team done for the day, pilot like some military hero, many of them handsome or just a shade off, the flight attendants all kinds now, women/men, old/young, gay/straight, the workers, most of them Hispanic or Native American here, cleaning the floors or trying to look busy. What I liked most was the sense of action and change. People were going places.

If anyone noticed me they didn't notice that I had no particular reason to be there, didn't care why I was there, why would they. I was just a guy in running clothes sweating either horribly or not so horribly depending on the weather. They didn't know and wouldn't care that I was training for the Olympics, that I had spent all morning and all afternoon submerged in an Olympic-sized swimming pool swimming laps, practicing my breaststroke and my butterfly, rubbing liniment into my legs and arms afterwards, secretly hating those big names who had made my Olympic career until now an impossibility—Lochte, Phelps, Berens. *Until now* because though I was old for a swimmer, nevermind how old, I was not about to give up. I was just hitting my stride. I just needed one or two people to get hurt and I would be in for Rio, and then watch out because I would give it my all to get the gold, I didn't care what it would take. I was one of those maniacally driven people and when that Olympic dream was realized or, heaven forfend, burst, I figured I would do just fine in any business of my choosing, selling nuclear waste to Third World countries maybe, or selling overpriced sportswear to high-end sportspeople or running a hotel, I didn't know what at that time but I figured I would figure it out.

She brushed my arm, the most incidental of contacts followed by a purposeful contact as she grabbed my forearm to excuse herself, and right then a surfeit of electricity passed through her fingers, a kind of sensual warmth, and she gripped my arm as if she were gripping a muscular snake. At the same time, we made eye contact, which is a strange phenomenon because it is so physical—you can actually *feel* someone looking at you. She looked like a strange Russian spy or a sinister femme fatale from a movie from my youth and at the same time like an uber-modern woman of the world, maybe a model comfortable in any kind of photo spread, this incredible woman like none I had ever seen before so that I believed my heart was going to literally burst, all of the clichéd love-at-first-sight scenes from movies suddenly making sense, an intense algorithm of chemicals or whatever. "I'm sorry," she said. "I'm also sorry," I said. "It's nothing," she said. I watched her walk away—she was wearing black skinny jeans beneath the suit jacket, wedges on her feet. Not dressed at all for the Southwestern climate, she was going to sweat like crazy out there; I imagined a drop of sweat rolling down her back. I imagined the barely-there whorls of hair on her back like lanugo on a baby, the tantalizingly beautiful descent of the sweatdrop between her shoulder blades, over the delicate knobs of her vertebrae, down to the curve of her lower back, where, respectfully, I didn't dare follow the trail any farther. I watched her walk away and I died more than a little. I see myself standing there, my smooth pate, my day-old stubble, my shaved arms, my running tights, lovelorn, torn apart by an incidental contact, and it seems to me that in that moment I represent a fundamental aspect of the human condition, experiencing, as I was, one of those emotions that is possible only in humans, something that can be called only yearning.

LATER, IN THE POOL, a moment of misidentification. Nikolai, my coach, was yelling at me as I struggled through the breaststroke, never my favorite, as I gasped air mixed with mist and rose above the water like some clumsy waterdragon, taking great gulps of air and willing fluidity, downhearted and muscle-fatigued, the day waning, the sun already passing across the frosted skylight as night was presaged in the pool, the long and slow Southwestern dusk just digging in its spurs, when I noticed a swimmer in the lane to my left. The pool was huge, of course, and mostly empty, but this swimmer had insisted on swimming in the lane directly adjoining mine. "Concentrate, Adrian," Nikolai shouted, apoplexied, "concentrate!" But how could I concentrate when the woman in the lane beside mine was passing me, also doing the breaststroke, as if mocking me, with perfect fluidity and torpedo speed? She hit the wall and dolphin-kicked, surfacing just to my left, and I glared at her, a difficult task with goggles over the eyes and the mouth gaping to catch another gasp of air. She was pinch-nosed, wearing a black cap, features indecipherable. I stopped swimming at the wall, clambered out to sit on the edge of the pool, Nikolai screaming something behind me, watched her emerge from the water at the far end and take off her cap, exposing her short black hair. I noticed that she was very tall, her shoulders broad—in the black swimsuit she didn't appear to have any breasts at all. My heartbeat clanged in my chest. Oh what a fool was I.

SHE WAS WAITING OUTSIDE the training facility, gym bag slung over one shoulder, wearing the same clothes she'd worn at the airport. Her hair so short it was almost dry already, black balls in her earlobes. I could smell the tang of shower soap, the ever-present perfume of chlorine, and the worsted wool suit jacket, which had collected her accretions for how long, though she didn't seem to be sweating now. I wiped my brow.

"You're a hell of a swimmer," I said. She shrugged, nodded, seemed pleased but didn't want to show it. "I'm thinking about giving up, after seeing you," I said, not realizing until I said it that it was actually true. My dreams of Olympic gold now seemed phantasms of a weak, a childish and a churlish mind. It was about time to pursue other career plans, which scared the bejesus out of me. I could see my future like a great gaping hole in the fabric of the universe, an unknown shape that, like a succubus, would come to consume me in the dark night. And I also saw it as something else, as a celebration of failure, as a fireworks display in an empty town, as mystery and goodness.

"You're not bad, exactly," she said, which only confirmed the decision.

"Maybe," I said. It was so easy to talk to her, the words so easy to wrangle, I didn't worry about shaming myself. "Can I show you the town?"

"Tomorrow," she said, touching my arm. She was about four inches taller than me, which meant she would be two inches taller than me without her shoes. Her touch was combustible. I watched her enter a cab, long legs folding up like a TV tray, eyes turning to look at me without any indication of what she might be thinking, a strange blank face like the face of one of those humanoid androids they like to develop in Japan. I realized that I was in trouble. My knees were weak as I shouldered my gym bag and walked down the dusty, dusky Albuquerque streets toward my hotel room, the place I had called home the last three years so I could train with Nikolai and dream stupid, unrealizable, now-embarrassing dreams. I'd never been good at anything except swimming, and I had been very good at that but not as good as the best in the world, which is probably the position of anyone who has ever tried to do anything in the world. There was this insurmountable barrier between good and great, and somehow I knew that I would never break through it, and the whole trick to living life now would be to determine how I could go on living with that fact.

When I lay in bed, it felt like I was still swimming, and I closed my eyes and imagined I was there in the water with her. She was carrying me through choppy waters, I was clinging to her strong shoulders, her nipples brushing mine, her strong arms carrying us into the middle of the ocean.

I wanted her to stop, but she couldn't or wouldn't and kept going. I masturbated, watched a bad movie, fell asleep.

WHAT DOES ONE DO when one loses one's compass in life? In which direction does one go? For a while, maybe, it's natural to continue in the same direction, pretending continued possession of a life that at one time seemed real and absolute. We wear our old clothes until we can afford to buy new ones. I awoke at four, ate my usual breakfast of granola mixed into plain yogurt, walked to the swimming facility, did my warm-up routine, jumped into the pool to swim laps while waiting for Nikolai to arrive and yell at me. The woman was already in the pool when I arrived, her long body a perfect instrument of aquatic gliding. During the morning the elderly do their p.t. in the other end of the pool and I stopped and watched them now and then. Their skin was oddly colored in the blue light that emanated up from the pool and the soft dawn light that filtered down through the skylights. Flesh of baby blues and pinks, mottled like alien skin. I could see the scalps of those who dared submerge their heads, their soft gray or white hair clamping down on them like creatures with tentacles. How sad their bodies but peaceful or even joyful their countenances. They could barely walk through the water, but they laughed, their laughter rippling down from the ceiling in overlapping echoes. I thought of babies swimming in wombs and our most ancient of ancestors breathing in the sea and how life was just a random accident in an immense and cold universe, but how warm and humane it could all seem, sometimes. I wanted to hug each and every one of the old people, but that would not go over well, especially since I had not shaved my arms, chest, face or scalp that morning and was a walking abrasion, a relatively lanky cut of sandpaper. Meanwhile, the woman continued to swim laps, a perfect form in the pool beside me.

Nikolai arrived, he yelled, I swam, I ran to the airport and back, ate lunch, trained again.

"You are bristly," Nikolai said halfway through the afternoon. "What is wrong with you, you don't shave?" I shrugged. He slapped me and stalked off, this squat out-of-shape bear of a little man with a bedhead hairstyle and a mustache. Impossible to believe he'd ever won a silver medal in the 1992 Olympics and had trained gold medalists. His khaki pants fit his lower half oddly—he waddled. I almost kind of loved him, maybe because I had grown up fatherless in Iowa and had never known anyone who cared about me enough to slap me, though he cared about me only because I was paying him with what was proving to be the dregs of a trust fund. I showered, dressing in the only dressy thing I owned, a short-sleeved checked shirt, blue jeans, cowboy boots I bought on a lark, as a laugh. I sat outside the facilities, sweating and remembering the friends I'd once had in high school and college before someone—my college coach—told me that I had a shot at the Olympics, how we had done things together, nothing earth-shattering, things like bowling and archery and getting crunk and looking for girls in random cities, how all that was over now, big deal, we move along in life whether we want to or not, and feeling all kinds of itchy.

She was wearing the same exact thing when she came out of the facilities—same suit jacket, same jeans, same wedges.

"If I ran my hand over your head, I would bleed," she said.

"Don't, then," I said.

She did a strange thing then. She grabbed my head and brought it close to her—I sniffed in the complex smellscape of her suit jacket—ran her hand over it, clutched it in both hands. Something maternal and caring and sexual all at once, rougher than expected.

"There, I did it. Take me to dinner."

I walked her into Old Town, where we could hear an Indian flute playing "The Wind Beneath My Wings," piped in through loudspeakers on every corner, the little adobe huts, almost all of them advertising "real authentic Indian jewelry," the sidewalks filled with tourists, men wearing bolos and concho belts and women in bright shirts, their asses like huge soft baked potatoes, a police officer wearing shorts and black boots. We walked into a shop and I bought her a turquoise necklace that she wore right away.

We ate at a place off the beaten track, with authentic New Mexican fare, green chile on everything, hot spicy shredded chicken and pork, drinking beer after beer, since I wasn't training in the morning and she didn't seem to care, and I told myself that I was not getting her drunk with impure intentions though clearly I was, even though she wasn't the kind of woman that anyone could ever take advantage of. We talked about our childhoods, mine in Iowa, hers in Maine, how pure childhood is, the way the mind of a child is pure even when it's not innocent, the TV shows we'd watched, the worlds we'd imagined, the ages we were when we first started swimming, how everything in the world came down to liquid.

"I want to shave you," she said. "You look uncomfortable." I shrugged, smiled, and a little later we were in the small hotel bathroom and she was shaving my chest, head, cheeks, arms. She shaved off my eyebrows, then oiled me up and we made love for what seemed like many athletic hours, with her almost always on top and my heart quaking as if it would give out, as if it had reached the promised land and nothing more beautiful or perfect could ever be expected so why bother.

MAYBE SENSING MY SWIMMING career had come to a sudden caesura, Nikolai left an angry resignation letter crumpled into the vent holes of my locker the next day. Instead of changing into my Speedo and donning my goggles, as planned, I walked out of the facilities and wandered around Albuquerque that morning, wending my way down narrow alleys, out to the river, past hand-painted murals dedicated to Jesus or Elvis Presley or both. The sky became leached of color as the day progressed. I had nothing to do and I did nothing until about eleven, when I ran fifteen miles down the Rio Grande and back before shaving, showering, having a nice lunch. The possibilities of life seemed both endless and nil. What now? I had a BA in Liberal Arts and no work history. I seemed in perfect condition for some kind of addiction that would tumble me into indigence and transience, maybe even intransigence, an eventuality that part of me hungered for, imagining the tang of real difficult living, struggle and whatnot. When I held Nat that night, I felt the warmth and heat of a long physical day. She seemed to be made up of hundreds of writhing snakes, each muscle another individual snake.

WEEKS PASSED IN THIS WAY, with running taking up an increasing amount of my time. I started training for a marathon, not in a competitive way because I thought I could win—I knew I couldn't—but because having something to train for had become ingrained, necessary as a hit of smack. The weather could be brutal, relentless sun cloudless skies, but the more relentless the more I liked it. I ran shirtless, became brown then bronze, my shoulder and chest muscles slowly atrophying. Sometimes when we made love she cried out in a strangled voice more real than anything I'd ever heard. It's difficult to encapsulate the affair, to say: this was what we did then, this was what she meant to me—but she meant more to me than I could ever explain. Because she trained so often, we did very little else except make love, lay in bed talking about our pasts but never our futures and only rarely our presents. She spent a lot of time on top of me.

My trust fund depleted, I got a fulltime job at the gas station across the street from the hotel. Wearing the blue coveralls felt odd at first, but it was just another uniform. I filled people's tanks without a word. After Nat left to train in Rio, an inevitability, something we never even talked about, I stopped shaving. Wearing the same thing she'd been wearing when she appeared—as if nothing about her had changed during those weeks—she said goodbye in the Sunport while I stood around in running pants, pieces of my inside being ripped out, gnawed over. It hurt deep, where all the strangest things in my life were stored, and I watched the plane take off without even knowing if it was hers. It ripped a hole right through me. Within a year I had grown a beard and my hair was long, tangled and salt and pepper. I lived in an adobe house just outside Old Town.

THREE YEARS AFTER WE MET, more than a thousand days later, I sat inside a minimally air-conditioned dive off Mountain Road, the wall unit clattering like some medieval torture device, an iron maiden or a rack, drinking a cold Corona quickly going warm, not *with* any of the locals at the bar but an accepted part of their daily visual terrain, looking up at the newly installed flat-screen TV close to the ceiling, watching a profile of her before her race, the two hundred meter butterfly first, which would be followed by the four-hundred-meter IM and the relay. She was "the bad girl of swimming" with her now multiple piercings and the tattoos of dragons racing down both arms, her hair dyed white at the tips. She'd grown up in a small town in Maine, where her mother struggled to make ends meet. She swam from the age of eight, and it was immediately apparent that she was something special, though no one expected her gifts to carry her this far. Feared, reviled, questioned—she had seen her share of controversy. Now she was ready to take it back, to prove to the world that she belonged here.

The locals watched impassively, the shirtless Mexican guy with tattoos who brought his dog into the bar with him, the white kid with the scraggly brown beard. I wanted to tell them that I knew her, that I had slept with her, but I wasn't that kind of guy, and the knowledge of what we'd known together kind of glowed inside me. During the end of the butterfly, she smashed her wrist against the wall of the pool, and during the medal ceremony she held her hand close to her chest—she didn't smile—the whole deal setting up a heroic leg of the relay, which no one thought she could really go through with, considering her injury, but which she basically won for the U.S. team. Everyone cheered (this was later, at another bar, closer to Old Town) and slapped each other on the back, chanting U.S.A., U.S.A. into the soft New Mexican night. I lugged myself home, listening to the cheers grow quieter.

AT NIGHT SOMETIMES NOWADAYS I will lay out in my backyard, which is nothing but a scurf of dirt with an old Oldsmobile rusting in one corner that was there when I bought the place and will be there when I die, looking up at all the stars and the billions of possibilities for life, and the Milky Way will seem like a warm stream of water across the sky. I'll imagine swimming it, arms oiled and churning, remembering the perfect equilibrium of the moment before having to worry about your hand hitting that wall.

Kavita

Kavita pedaled toward her aunt's house. Her legs ached from dance class, the only high school class she enjoyed. The sky was gnarled up. The woods beside the road were thick with young pine trees, but she could also smell ocean marsh. She stopped pedaling, removed her hands from the handlebars, let the weight of her backpack, the weight of her body, gravity and entropy, carry her forward. A body in motion. An equal and opposite force. Her feet dangled. She had a strong, dancer's body, thick at the hips and thighs, forceful. She was always aware of her center, just below the navel. She let go of the center. The thin bicycle tire jagged on dirt beside the road. She landed heavily on her side, her leg scraping across the ground, in tall dry grass, the trunks of pine trees sideways, as if growing out of a dim green wall.

A man came to her as she lay still. The gnarled sky unfurled, dropping hard black drops of rain. Her aunt would wonder where she was, would send police officers out to look for her. They would sweep the roadside with searchlights calling her name. Kavita. The man was a light-skinned black man wearing thick, black-framed glasses and a black suit. His white shirt glowed. Everything about him was immaculate. The man reached out to touch her leg, gripped her thigh in his palm. Her leg was muscular, tight, his grip strong.

"Come on, now, Kavita," he urged. "Get up."

The rain intensified, lifting the smell of swamps and sulfur from the earth. Hell. Her father was in Hell. The man regarded her with curiosity, distrust, disappointment, it was hard to tell which. She would stay on the ground forever. She would let the rough grass grow over her. Her heart would sink into the black mud and beat there. She breathed because she did not know how to stop breathing. The man cradled her head against his chest, her wet hair dirtying his white shirt.

"Come on, now," the man said, his voice her father's calm deep voice. "It's okay."

Two lights from the road rippled across the grass. Gnats rose from the ground. She felt them biting her shoulders her face her legs and the depression where her neck met her chest. The car did not stop. Kavita blinked. There was no man, no man's footprints. She lifted herself, then the bicycle. She walked down the road, the rim of the front tire warped now, describing a wayward rhythm.

"what happened to your leg?"

Her aunt was divorced. Her aunt's two children played in the scurfy grass behind the ranch house. The rain had ended. Kavita watched them through the window, wondered what game they were playing. The boy whipped a long thin branch through wet grass. The girl crouched, watching him. There was an intensity to their game, a seriousness.

"Nothing."

"Nothing, Kavita? Look at it. It looks like raw meat. You should wash it out."

"I will."

Her aunt had left Trinidad three years before her parents had. She had married a white man, an American. Her children were U.S. citizens. Outside, both children were now crouched before something Kavita could not see. A dead animal, she assumed. A brown and gray unidentifiable body.

She washed her leg in the white tub, rubbing off particles of dirt, road, and pebbles. The water ran pink down the ringed drain; the falling pebbles made small sounds like insects chewing. This was real: the blood, her leg, the pain. Her body would heal itself. The water ran cold, then warm, then hot. Steam clouded the mirror. When she looked inside, her reflection ghosted. A man stood behind her wearing a black suit, a white shirt. She watched the rise and fall of her chest. He would grab her neck with both of his hands. Her neck was strong. It would not be easy for him. With her fingertip, she traced her outline in the mirror, her broad shoulders, her square head, her snaking hair, her waist. This is me. Kavita. You cannot kill me.

THEN:

Her life had been held up by a pillow of air. She moved through that life effortlessly. She knew she was lucky but not that she was privileged. Dance lessons, sleepovers, movies, her large home in Ridgewood. Her room, her television, her computer.

She sat down to dinner with her mother and father, laughing, explaining her life to them, showing them almost all of it. Petty trouble with friends, her first kiss. Her father was often tired, but he smiled as he listened.

None of this was real.

TO KAVITA, DANCING WAS JOY, but not in an easy or a simple way. Joy was possible in the world, but it had to be earned. Her body was the source of joy. Her legs were strong, her sense of rhythm very good, her weight centered. She felt movement in her muscles even without music. The dance teacher at the high school, Beth, was young, white, petite, her light blue eyes rimmed with thick black mascara. She was not always capable of controlling the class. On the dance team, power was contested. Kavita tried to stay in the background but was too good to remain invisible.

"Kavita, that's beautiful," Beth said. "Perfect."

Dancing was hard work, yes, but every move was perfectable. Eventually any move could be repeated with precision.

Dancing was also grueling. It was sweat and exhaustion.

Sometimes joy was not welcome. How can you feel this, now? She hid everything from her classmates. She smiled and laughed often. They were all strangers. She just needed to get through this year. Then: college. New life. Forgetting. People liked her. Teachers liked her, most of the other girls on the dance team liked her, boys liked her. It was not Ridgewood.

After school she did her homework at the kitchen table, or, if her aunt was not home from the hospital where she worked yet, played with the children. The boy was hard on the girl, pushing her down, smearing her face with dirt, but the girl was tough. Kavita danced with them in the backyard, gave them twirling ribbons on sticks. They ran through the grass laughing. Afterwards she would check them for ticks, carefully picking the insects out where they had rooted into the skin, sure to remove legs and teeth.

The man appeared only when she was alone, so Kavita tried to never be alone. He was always behind her, wearing a jackal's smile. He sat beside her bed at night, touching her forehead.

"Come on, now, Kavita. It's not so bad."

When she slept, she often had nightmares, but they disappeared as soon as she woke. The man's white shirt glowed in the dark room.

"KAVITA? WHAT KIND OF NAME IS THAT?"

"It's Trini. I'm Trini."

"You don't look Trini."

"That's what people tell me all the time, but I am." She smiled, her white teeth straight after years of braces. Full lips. Be beautiful.

Tim leaned toward her. His skin was the color of hot chocolate, his cheeks angular. He wore his hair short, but it seemed to grow quickly—he was always in need of a shape up. His arms were thin and smooth. Trouble, people said. What did people know?

"Man, I think it's just beautiful, though. Kavita." He tasted the name.

"Really? Thanks."

"Beautiful name, beautiful name." They were supposed to be translating Shakespeare into modern English. A sonnet. My lover's eyes are nothing like the sun. Wasn't that English already? She moved her fingers along the edge of the paper, watching her wrist. Strong forearm, thin wrist, smooth dark skin. Do you see my hand? Do you see me?

"I haven't seen you anywhere around. Parties. Don't you go to parties, girl? Don't you like parties?"

"Sometimes."

"Sometimes? You don't like to have a good time? I can tell you like to have a good time. Look at that smile. I'm right, right?" She shrugged, smiled. Games. Coded dances. "I'll pick you up nine o'clock, Friday."

"Okay."

"Okay?"

"Okay." She nodded, smiled, turned away from him.

THEN:

In many ways, she was old enough to be a woman but was a child still. Her father had yelled before. He had thrown glasses across the room, sudden explosions. Shards. He had complained about his economics students at the university, about how cold Americans were. He had brooded. It was what fathers did.

Every day she walked home from the high school, a few blocks, down safe, tree-lined streets, with friends. They laughed, made plans for the weekend. Every day she walked into her house, hugged her mother, drank a glass of orange juice.

She noticed blood on the tile floor. Her mind struggled to fit the blood into her schema of home. Someone had gotten hurt. Were they alright? Her mother's body was draped across the kitchen counter, a gash in her center, blood matting her black hair. Her father's body was slumped against the French doors, blood and brains spattered across the glass. None of this was real. All of this was real. She stood at the entrance to the kitchen, her backpack in her hand. She had Algebra homework. Algebra was difficult for her. She was hoping her father would help her understand. The handgun her father had shown her once—"for protection," he had said—had fallen on the tile floor, away from his clutched hand. His face was gone.

She answered the questions asked of her. She rode in the back of her aunt's car. She was alive. I am still alive, she wanted to tell them. Her father had worn black suits, pristine white shirts.

KAVITA DRESSED IN A TIGHT black t-shirt that stretched across her chest, a bright yellow overshirt, a skirt, gladiator sandals. She didn't know how to dress. Her aunt looked at her.

"Going out tonight, Kavita?"

"Yes."

"Good for you."

Her aunt had taken her own grief and tucked it inside of her. A sachet. Her aunt was kind, but she would not allow her soul dominion over her body. All life was risk. Didn't she see that?

The party was loud and crowded, in a large house near a small pond. Tim held her hand, handed her a drink.

"I don't drink," she told him.

"What do you mean you don't drink?" He smiled but was not happy.

"I don't drink."

"What do you do then? Do you smoke?"

"No. I dance."

The music was loud, the bodies pressed close against each other. In Ridgewood she had gone to parties, danced with her girlfriends, flirted with boys, laughed. Here the music was loud, everyone drank, couples were already in corners kissing.

"Can we go outside?"

"Girl, I need to get a drink."

Kavita walked out of the house. The pond had once been a cranberry bog, and just below the surface she saw overgrown cranberry bushes with red branches like hair.

SHE WALKED DOWN LONG empty dark roads, pine trees on either side of her. The wind picked up, blowing her yellow shirt in different directions, a flag flapping. She was iron and wood. When the man in the black suit and white shirt made his appearance this time, she decided, she was going to talk to him. She was going to tell him that she was done with him. She didn't want to see him ever again. He would not leave her—she knew he wouldn't—but she could be done with him.

A Wolf at the Door

Geraldine opened the door and looked out at the wolf standing on the front porch. It was a large wolf, wild, and there was no way it could have knocked on the door. Still, a knock had roused her from her nap, she had crossed the living room floor to open the front door, and there it stood. Its teeth were bared, its ears pinned back to its head, and a low growl emanated from its throat. It was a horrifying sight, but before she felt fright Geraldine felt confusion. How could this wild wolf have found its way here, to Forest Park, a residential neighborhood in West Baltimore? It was no place for wolves, certainly not for wolves of this size or ferocity. In her fifteen years in Forest Park, Geraldine had seen foxes and raccoons, and once she had found a large buck standing on the front lawn, but a wolf? It was absurd. She had a hard time believing it, though there it was.

She looked first one way, then the other. There was no one around to testify to the presence of the wolf. She turned away to close the door, unwilling to put up with this foolishness, but that was when the animal, the beast, lunged toward her, its mouth opening much wider than seemed possible. She saw its reddish gums, its sharp yellowed teeth, the red tunnel of its throat, and she felt the darkness descend all around her—was the wolf really swallowing her whole? She felt a strangeness along the edges of her body, a viscous squeezing, pressure against her head and sides, and then she was somehow looking through the wolf's eyes, seeing everything the way a wild animal would. She felt a kind of hunger she'd never felt before, a will to destroy, to eat the whole world until it was broken down inside her powerful guts. A frightening yet oddly familiar feeling.

She was left with the afterglow of that sensation when she opened her eyes from her nap and heard the knock at the door a second time, louder now, more insistent. It was an echo of what just happened in what she told herself had to have been a dream—though it felt more real than any dream she'd ever had. She walked across the living room floor toward the door, resting her hand on the doorknob an extra beat before opening it. She refused to be afraid—Geraldine was not a fearful woman. She fully expected the wolf to be standing on the other side of the door, though another part of her knew who it was, who it had to be, knocking on her door like that. Richard.

And it was Richard, the brother who was five years her junior. He'd never had any patience, even when they were children, and what patience he'd once had had raveled out of existence after years of drug abuse and bad, and she meant *bad*, relationships. Mutually abusive. Now he stood on Geraldine's porch wearing all navy blue—loose navy blue pants, a navy blue jacket over a navy blue t-shirt, even navy blue New Balance sneakers.

"Richard. What do you want?" Too groggy for niceties. And that feeling from the dream... it was still with her. Muted now, but there.

"You called me."

"Mm. I must have dozed off."

"Must have."

Though only five years separated them, they seemed to belong to different generations. While Richard clung to his youth with a tenacity that would have been admirable if it didn't make him foolish, Geraldine had already crested the hill and was over it.

She couldn't recall calling Richard but knew she must have, and she gradually remembered why she must have and led him down the stairs, toward the street. The yard of the house was generous, but the landlord didn't care for it well. Now the yard was covered with rotting leaves under piles of melted snow. It was very cold out, and Geraldine wore only the sparkly silver slacks and white top with the elaborate bow at the bust she'd put on earlier that day to drive to the shelter where she volunteered. A holiday party. She'd brought four different kinds of cookies.

She had been volunteering at the shelter for only a few months but already felt like part of the community. They welcomed her by name. She loved it there, though she also loved being able to leave.

"Well," she said. "There it is."

The car was a Centro Lobo she'd purchased less than a year earlier, a simple black sedan that caused her undue pride when she first bought it. It replaced her twenty-year-old battered Subaru. For a few months the new car had been pristine, a sleek black vehicle she cleaned at the Sudsville every Sunday after church. Then she had come out of the grocery store one morning to find the passenger side of the car scraped up. It had been like someone ran a cheese grater across her own face; it hurt that much. But that was the sin of pride, and she refused to pay the deductible that would have been charged had she contacted her insurance company.

She found a way to live with the scrapes. It was possible to ignore them if she parked the car a certain way. Then, a few weeks ago, someone had driven by on the street in the middle of the night and smashed her two driver's side windows out. For three days she'd driven with cellophane taped over the windows, flapping everywhere she drove, until finally she had the windows repaired. Richard knew a man who worked on cars on the spot, and he charged only three quarters of what the official places would have. She paid him less than her deductible.

Now this.

This was a broken grille. Looking at it made the feeling from her dream, the world-eating feeling, vibrate at the edge of her perception.

The deer leapt out of the woods by the side of the road as she was driving back from the shelter that morning, giving her no warning. There was a stretch of woods between Forest Park and the shelter, an urban wilderness as deep as urban wilderness got, tree trunks growing thick. There was nothing she could do but brace for impact. *Wham.* She'd hit the flank of the animal, which skittered on the wet road before hobbling back into the forest from whence it came. For some reason (probably shoddy workmanship) the airbag of the Centro had not deployed, and Geraldine bashed her head against the windshield. At least she was pretty sure that's what happened. The windshield appeared uninjured, but she remembered being hurtled forward, and then she remembered settling back in the driver's seat and looking around her. She did not remember the moment of impact, but that didn't mean it hadn't happened. Her head hurt and her thoughts were cloudier than usual. So there was that.

"It looks like you were lucky," Richard said, crouching to inspect the damage.

"Oh really. Lucky?"

"Yeah. Lucky. It's just the grille. Radiator's fine. Airbag didn't even go off. I can get you a grille from a junkyard. Replace it myself for two hundred."

Geraldine nodded and hummed deep in her throat. If Richard was charging her two hundred, that meant it would cost him ten, if not less. She figured it was a handy way to give Richard money without him having to ask for it, but she hoped it wasn't going to be used for whatever drug he had moved onto now. Coke, heroin, oxy, meth. She was pretty sure he'd gone through every one. She'd let him live with her for three months, about five years ago now, and still regretted that decision. Never again. He'd stolen from her shamelessly. He'd shown up at the house at two or three a.m., making a lot of noise, yelling into his cellphone at his abusive girlfriend of the moment, and it was a respectable house. She had apologized to her neighbors and kicked him out after the allotted three months were up. He'd never asked to come back, but he sometimes asked for money.

She looked at the thick gray, tan, and white hairs embedded in what remained of the grille. Blood dotted one corner. She wondered if the deer survived and felt a swelling of hunger, as if she wanted to pursue that poor animal, hunt it down, fall on it, and eat it raw, starting at its tender neck. She imagined blood spuming into her open mouth, then shook her head. That was an image out of another mind, somehow, not hers. She remembered the wolf that stood at the door in her dream and the way he'd eaten her whole.

"I'll get the grille today, be back tomorrow morning to put it in. You'll have the money?"

"I'll have the money, Richard."

"You okay?" he asked her. She realized she'd been staring at the fur embedded in the grille. She turned to her brother and smiled.

"Don't I seem okay?"

"I don't know. I guess."

They hugged, and Richard left in the old Subaru beater she'd given him for nothing when she bought the new car. Nothing was what it was worth. Now there was a hole in its muffler and it rattled loud down the street.

She often hated Richard, often acted as if he was not her brother. They'd grown up on the edge of Edmonson Village, near the cemetery. She had stayed out of trouble, while he dove headlong into it. When she was ten their mother started leaving her in charge of Richard, and sometimes she felt as much like a mother to him as a sister. At first, he had minded her, but by the time he was ten there was no controlling him. He ran wild. She had no idea what he really did in the streets.

As soon as she could, she'd gone away to Morgan State, right across town but far enough that it felt like another world.

Sometimes she felt like Richard's failed life, and it couldn't be classified as anything other than that, was her fault. She should have been stricter with him, should have figured out a way to make him mind, should have tied him to the chair in the living room if it came to that. Should have saved him from himself. She still remembered when she found him in the cemetery at six o'clock on a winter evening. It was already dark. Her mother had sent her out to fetch him, and she hadn't really expected to find him, but something led her into the cemetery. He was so drunk he was curled up on top of a pile of his own vomit, barely conscious. He was ten years old then, and she was worried he was going to die. Back at the apartment their mother stripped Richard and bathed him, like she did when they were babies, then put him in a sweatsuit and held him on the couch, running her fingers over his forehead. Geraldine had felt more jealous than she'd ever felt in her life.

After Richard left, she went inside her apartment and lay back down. She didn't like to nap during the day, but she was still so tired. When she woke this time, she couldn't remember her dreams but still felt the strange earth-eating feeling of a wolf. She saw a package of lamb steak defrosting in the sink. She didn't remember getting the meat out of the freezer, but she must have taken it out right after returning to the apartment following the accident. She tore into the plastic, seasoned the meat with peppercorns and sea salt. Some of the blood got on her fingers and she found herself licking it off.

She turned on her stereo, an old system with a CD player, and put on the Ohio Players, listened as she grilled the lamb, then sat at the table and scarfed the meal down, though it couldn't properly be called a "meal." She was used to being alone now. She'd been married for only two years. A good two years. Roland had always been so sweet and kind to her. They'd even tried to have children, or at least she had. She'd not been all that surprised when Roland came out of the closet and left her and, despite the pain they both endured, they were still friends. He was much happier now. She couldn't say the same, but that was no one's fault.

The steak was not enough, and Geraldine found herself rooting around the refrigerator. There were angus burgers in the freezer, and she fried one up and ate it, sat feeling deeply satiated, listening to an old Mahalia Jackson CD, one she hadn't listened to in years. It sounded good but wild, the great woman's voice rising and rising and never cracking. "Didn't It Rain?"

She felt as if the music was warring in her soul with the feeling that had been with her ever since she'd woken from her nap, the mad hunger. She would not nap the next day, that was for sure. Maybe she would never nap again.

She dressed in her velour sweatsuit, purple with white piping up each leg, settled in the living room with a blanket to watch her programs, a drama featuring a multicultural cast, a comedy, the news, treated herself to a hot toddy, then went to bed early.

She found herself crossing the bedroom at early o'clock, two or three a.m., fuzzy slippers afoot. It had to be Richard again, knocking at this time. She was disappointed in him but not surprised. He was probably going to try to get the two hundred dollars from her early so he could buy whatever he thought would soothe his soul. He was going to look gruff, unshaven, and angry, all rent up the way he got when his need grew too great. She was surprised Richard had never spent time in prison. Maybe that was what he needed. She had contemplated it in the past: ratting on him, but the no-snitching ethic she'd grown up with had gotten into her psyche and could not be dislodged.

She put on her disappointed face as she opened the door. But instead of Richard, it was the wolf, returned. No, it was another wolf, one that looked related to the first. It was bigger, maybe, or sleeker, or its eyes were a different color. It was the mate of the first, maybe. They locked eyes, then the wolf turned and walked slowly down the stairs. It stood on the walkway waiting until Geraldine put on her coat and hat, changed out her fuzzy slippers for snow boots, and walked outside after it.

The walkway was almost frozen solid, and Geraldine walked cautiously. The wolf circled her, its huge paws spreading on the ice. On the second floor of the house, she heard Marian's dog, Snowball, barking loud and frenzied, and she felt bad for waking the whole neighborhood up.

She opened the door of the Lobo for the wolf. It climbed into the passenger seat and sat like a good dog while she got behind the steering wheel, put her seatbelt on, and drove across town. She remembered how she felt yesterday morning while heading to the shelter. It had been clear and cold and she had felt good about everything. She was going to bring four different kinds of cookies to people in need. She didn't think of them that way—at least she tried not to. They were just people. Anyone could be in their position. She herself could be in that position, though she never had been. She'd earned her degree at Morgan and worked for the city ever since. She'd moved up, level after level, and was now able to save money. A considerable amount. She could buy a new car if it were that important to her. She noticed now, as she drove through the darkness, a hairline crack in the windshield where she must have hit her head. She didn't remember it from earlier. She turned to look at the wolf in the passenger seat, expecting it not to be there, but the wolf looked back at her, its mouth open, a warm gamy odor emanating from between its yellow teeth. Its gums were black.

She parked the car on the side of the road where the urban wild grew thickest. In the dark it seemed even thicker. She popped the hazard lights on and opened the passenger door for the wolf. It—it was a "she," she noticed—started sniffing the broken grille and the roadside. The trail of blood seemed to shine with a kind of phosphorescence. Geraldine could smell it, too, a rich iron-drenched scent. She followed the wolf into the woods. She was able to move faster than before, her muscles supple. She felt her limbs carrying her forward, the trees appearing before her then passing behind her. She navigated around them with unerring accuracy. There was nothing to fear here, only things to eat. She was an apex predator. She was the queen of the woods. And she was hungry.

They came upon the injured deer in a copse several miles into the woods. It lay on its side breathing heavily. It was a beautiful, injured thing. Its ribcage rose and fell. Its black nose was wet and shone in the moonlight. They descended onto it as one, rending muscle from bone. She heard the deer make a sound she'd never heard before, a kind of existential cry, carrying a fear of death she didn't know wild animals possessed. She felt the blood warm on her neck and chin, and she exulted in it.

IN THE MORNING SHE WOKE IN BED, sun shining through the blinds. The velour sweatsuit she wore was encrusted with blood and she smelled the rich scent of carrion coming from her own body. She'd smelled dead deer in the woods before (not that she went into the woods often) but not a recently dead deer. It had a sweet musk to it. She buried the bloody sweatsuit under a pile of dirty clothes in the laundry basket to deal with later and took a long hot shower. In the bathroom mirror, her face seemed to have narrowed a fraction. Her eyes held a steeliness they hadn't before.

She made extra eggs, extra bacon, and extra toast, and she was not surprised when she looked out her front window and saw Richard at work replacing the grille on her car. He was no mechanic, and he would do a poor job, but she didn't particularly care.

When he was finished, he knocked on the door and she let him in. He treated her house like a guest who'd once been a tenant, looking around with a proprietary air. He tucked into the eggs as if he hadn't eaten in days, a distinct possibility. She looked at him, trying to determine if he was high on something, or coming down from something, or trying to get off of something, but she had no idea. Some of the people at the shelter were addicts, too; she realized she afforded them a kind of grace she didn't afford her own brother. She assumed their addictions were not their fault, while, to her, his was his and his alone.

When he was almost finished with the eggs, he sniffed and looked around.

"Damn. What is that?"

"What is what?"

"That smell?'

"I don't know what you're referring to."

"There's a smell in here. God…"

He shook his head, finished the meal, sipped his coffee. She could tell he was trying to ignore the smell but was unable to. She handed him two hundred dollars in twenties, and he shoved it into his pocket without looking at it. He'd never tried to break into her house. He'd stolen things without remorse when he was living with her, but they were always small things, things she wouldn't miss. He knew where she kept her money and could have cleaned her out if he'd wanted to. He could easily have come in and stolen everything.

"I love you, Richard."

"Where the hell did that come from?" he said, looking at her. The words seemed to shake him as much as the smell did.

"I just wanted you to know."

"Oh. Okay. I love you too, Sis."

He left, well-fed, the two hundred dollars in the pocket of his navy blue pants. She wondered what he would do with the money.

ALL DAY SHE WAITED FOR THE WOLF to appear at her door, for them to go out again, hunting down their next prey, but it didn't. It didn't come back the next night or the night after that, and after a while she realized that it had been a one-time thing. She was worried about the state of her soul because the events had been so real. It had not been a dream but a spiritual truth.

While she watched her programs, while she made large meals that she would freeze, while she cleaned her apartment, she would wait for that feeling again. She ached for it.

SHE ATTENDED RICHARD'S FUNERAL wearing black slacks and a black blouse with an elaborate bow at the bust. He was dressed in a navy blue button-up shirt and dark blue jeans, and he resembled a doll. He'd ODed on fentanyl and been found in the Subaru a few streets over from where they grew up. There were many attendees at the funeral, dozens of people Richard's age and younger, but Geraldine didn't know a single one. At least three women carried on as if they had lost husbands. Or fathers.

She thought about what it meant to be strong, what it meant to be part of a family, part of a pack.

He was buried in the cemetery outside Edmondson Village.

WHEN THE NEXT ACCIDENT OCCURRED, when the Centro was finally totaled, it was almost exactly a year later. It had snowed the night before. Then it rained, and the rain cleared away the snow, but the morning was cold and icy. She was bringing a bag of her old clothes to the shelter. She planned to spend time with some of the women she'd become close with since she started volunteering. There was Gladys, who looked fifteen years older than her, with her toothless grin and wrinkled face, but was in fact the same age. There was Theresa, who liked to play Yahtzee and cheated like a snake. There was Albertine, who had frizzy white hair that stuck straight up like Don King. Geraldine looked forward to seeing them and was possibly a little preoccupied as she drove.

The car coming toward her on the road swerved to avoid another car sliding in from a side street, and then it was spinning, coming straight toward her. Geraldine found herself smiling, felt her eyes go hard like two brilliant pebbles, felt the hunger to break and eat the entire world come back and course through her. She waited for it with all her muscles tensed. Whatever happened, she was ready for it.

Whippet

It's 2:11 a.m. when I get out of bed and pace around what was once my uncle's bedroom, the baseball-sized scab on my scalp itching like a son of a bitch. The room is small, square, and crammed full of decades of my grandparents' stuff—hundreds of glossy crocheting magazines, homemade afghans in soft stacks that reach the ceiling, doodads on the dresser, including a dried baby crocodile, brittle and brown with matte black eyeballs. The frame of the crocodile's body is reinforced with wire, its teeth are tiny and yellow, and I wonder where they got it anyway. This early in the morning the crocodile seems almost alive, and all I want to do is get away from it. There's nothing to do but go downstairs and make myself some of my grandmother's herbal tea.

Grandma is awake, too. She sits in her easy chair in the parlor, a thick white nightgown blanketing her body, her head looking shrunken, pale blue light shining from her eyes.

"So," she says, "how's the convalescent?"

"Don't you ever sleep?"

"Not anymore."

The dog, a Shih Tzu, doesn't sleep either, and now he hops off Grandma's lap, where he'd blended in with the nightgown, and follows at my heels. The dog is mute. During the day he sits on the kitchen table mime-barking for long hours. He probably had a name at one point, but now everyone just calls him "dog." When I get around the corner, I kick at his muzzle a little. He crouches on his forepaws and acts like he's growling, but all you can hear is the tic-tacking of his scrabbly nails. When I pull my foot back again, the dog hauls ass back to Grandma.

"What did you do to him?" she calls.

"Nothing," I yell back. Raising my voice makes pain pump into my head, which is like a kid's science experiment on pressure. Sometimes it feels like it's floating off of my neck, and sometimes it feels like it's splitting open. The scab is one constant itch. I figure that's a good thing, that it means I'm healing properly.

Even though it's been a month since I moved in with my grandmother, I'm still not used to the house, how things are arranged in it, so I have to root behind the Ovaltine for a couple minutes before I come up with the Celestial Seasonings.

My grandfather's been dead for ten years, and my grandmother never complained about living alone until she saw a fat man wandering around the block holding a butcher's knife with a "dazed expression" on his face. At a family meeting it was decided that I was most expendable because of various things that had happened—job loss, for instance. So here I am. I haven't seen anything suspicious in the neighborhood yet, but I try to be on my guard. It's an old neighborhood in a Massachusetts mill city, and when some elderly German or Irish person dies a young immigrant family will move into their empty tenement apartment.

Most of my days are spent looking across the street at the nice-looking women in black nylons passing in and out of the doors of the Kingdom Hall, where the Jehovahs meet. The Kingdom Hall is squat and made of brick, with two wide smoked-glass doors. Once in a while I mow the lawn or hose down the walkway or drive to the drugstore to pick up Grandma's prescriptions. It's not a bad arrangement.

I microwave a mug of water, drop in the almond tea bag.

"One good thing about the head," Grandma says when I sit down on the sofa in the parlor. "Your hair'll grow in fuller."

"If it comes in at all."

"There has never been a bald Woodhall," she says. "Never." I wonder if it's true, and what it means if it is.

We sit for a while.

The next day, I sit on the steps of the front porch, looking away from the Kingdom Hall and up a steep hill of tenement houses. When my grandfather was alive he'd had a regular schedule for painting the porch. Every year he slathered the porch with thick sweeps of maroon. After his death my grandmother decided that white was the order of the day, so she hired someone to slap even thicker white paint over the maroon. Now the white is dirty and chipped in high-traffic areas, and the maroon shows through. Things are getting ugly. The lattice has seen better days. At interstices, the wood is rotting, the staples have iodized and then blackened, and whatever vines were growing up the lattice when I was a kid aren't anymore. I have a headache like demonic possession—wicked and unshakable. Even thinking about doing something is too much for me, so I just look at the neighborhood.

On the street just in front of my grandmother's driveway, a squat Hispanic man seems to materialize, his chest and shoulders popping up from the asphalt. He walks back and forth, steamed. My senses prick up: danger. He crosses the street and paces in front of that house, the house where, when I was a kid, the Bananos lived. The Bananos didn't celebrate Halloween, and the children always wore black, formal clothes. A perpetual wake. But in back of the house they'd had an in-ground pool, and sometimes I'd catch sight of part of the body of one of them, in a bathing suit, jumping into the water. I figured there were at least two worlds across the street that I would never understand.

"Just look at that Puerto Rican," my grandmother says when she pushes open the screen door and steps onto the porch, gripping two glasses of lemonade. She's still wrapped in her white robe. In the sunlight she looks older and out of place. Systems and subsystems of wrinkles are inscribed on what's exposed of her porous skin. Grandma was once a burlesque dancer in Boston—a big family secret that everyone knows—who called herself Red Ruby the Oyster Girl. She'd hopped out of a clam in heels and showed her gams. My grandfather met her, wooed her, carried her away from her seedy life and brought her to the mill city. Then he got her pregnant and went off to war. She still retains a hint of her former beauty, a sense of style.

"He hasn't done anything yet," I say.

"Who knows, who knows."

She hands me my lemonade and goes back inside, where she stands, arms crossed, glaring out the window. The dog mime-barks on the kitchen table. Grandma's face is immobile, carved with worry and hate, like a bowsprit. Eventually the guy walks away and I hear him yelling at someone down the street in Spanish.

"Close one," I say to Grandma behind the window, giving the thumbs-up. She doesn't hear me, she doesn't see me.

IT'S BEEN ABOUT THREE MONTHS since I worked any kind of job. My brother is an art professor, my sister married a sports analyst, my cousins are things like electrical engineers. Life seems to veer out of control sometimes, like the clock at Pizza Hut with the second hand that just flies around the face. One minute you're working your usual job, winding transformers, which might not be much but is something, and the next minute you're laid off. Eventually unemployment runs out. You're too old and you have no skills that make any sense anymore. Right now I'm recouping, I'm planning, I'm getting the big picture into focus.

When I have nothing else to do I lie in my uncle's old bed fingering the dead baby crocodile. It seems like an artifact from a simpler world, a world where nobody wondered whether it was right or wrong to kill and stuff baby crocodiles for tourists. A world where nobody knew smoking caused cancer. A world where somebody could learn something and just do it for the rest of their life.

LATER IN THE DAY GRANDMA puts on a flowery black shirt that has a complicated front of folds and strings that I'm pretty sure she hasn't secured properly, white slacks and cream-colored half-pumps. Her ankles look enormous, like four baked potatoes in abnormally brown nylons.

"I want you to meet Henry Screw," she says. That can't possibly be his name, but I don't ask her to repeat it.

"Sounds good," I say.

"Henry is a friend of mine."

"I figured. Should I change?" I'm wearing a light tan Allman Brothers t-shirt I found in the drawer of my uncle's old dresser, covering his stash of *Playboy*s from the 1970s, women with huge breasts shot in soft focus, horses and willow trees. The shirt smells like old wood and has a number of runs.

"Shut up, you," Grandma says.

Henry Screw lives across the street, in the only single-story house in the neighborhood, next to the Kingdom Hall. A fence separates his yard from the side parking lot, but Henry has made a square hole in the fence and he's sitting on a lawn chair in a scurf of weeds in front of the hole, drinking a beer. He wears black socks and brown sandals, Florida retiree gear. He lifts his ankles to scratch viciously now and then.

"Hey," Henry says. "There she is."

"Here I am all right," Grandma says.

We pull up two lawn chairs. It seems okay that no one introduces me. After a while, Henry looks over.

"The spics use your head for a baseball or something?" he says.

"Don't even talk about it," my grandmother says, then laughs. Henry laughs with her.

"Here," Henry says. He throws two beers at the same time, the cans making lazy parabolic trajectories into our hands. We open them, and I drain half of mine right away, even though I know, with the head, that it's a bad idea. Henry hasn't looked away from the hole in the fence for more than a few seconds at a time, but he doesn't seem interested in what's happening over there, which is just a couple people going in and coming out.

"Not what it used to be," Henry says.

"You can say that again."

After a while I hear keening coming from Henry's house.

"Let the dog out, will you," he says.

When I open the back screen door of the ranch-style house, a small animal rushes past me. It's like a greyhound, but much smaller. It starts circling the little yard, moving too fast for me to tell whether it's gray or brown.

"Whippet," Henry says.

"Right." I sit back down and count the revolutions; I stop when I get to a hundred. I grab another beer from a Styrofoam cooler near Henry's chair. "Smoke 'em if you got 'em," he says. I nod.

"You mow this lawn once a month, I'll pay you twenty bucks," he says.

"You're on."

He nods and grins like he's just conducted a shrewd business deal.

After a while Grandma goes into the house with Henry and I'm left alone with the dog in the side yard. I squinch over to where Henry was sitting before, knocking his chair out of the way, so I can watch the good looking women in black nylons. Maybe I should leave, but Henry's beer is good. I try not to picture what's happening in the house behind me.

Ten years from now, there won't be anyone like my grandmother or Henry Screw living in this neighborhood. Their houses will be torn down and tenements or apartment buildings will be put up. Maybe they'll turn Henry's place into additional parking for the Kingdom Hall. The lot is too small now and Jehovahs park up and down the street and walk all over the sidewalks. On certain days, the whole street smells like dry-cleaned clothes and perfume.

The whippet falls asleep balled on my lap. The itching of the scab, which had been crazy when I'd first started with the beer, goes away. I can anticipate what it will feel like tomorrow: fire, cracking, bleeding pain. At this point it's best to keep drinking.

I go back to my grandmother's house with two of Henry's beers. In my uncle's old room, I leaf through old *Playboys*, but it feels more like research for something I don't want to do than enticement. The lesbian scenes are all intimation. Everything is so soft I feel woozy. I pick up the dried baby croc again. It crackles to the touch and seems like something somebody would pray to, something with a soul still in it. I put it on my chest and lie like that for a while. The crocodile seems to communicate something to me. I can't put it into words exactly, but it has something to do with getting up, getting out, being young, taking action.

I borrow my grandmother's El Dorado and drive across the state line, back to my old hometown. I drive past the homes of all the people I once knew, wondering if any of them are unlucky enough to still live there. In front of the house of somebody I hardly knew, there's Bob Worthington watering his lawn, or his parents' lawn. He's wearing shorts cuffed around his fat thighs and his thumb is jammed in the hose opening, creating a fanspray of water.

I raise my hand and he raises his back, but I can tell he doesn't recognize me.

Girls I had crushes on, guys who beat me up, people I hated and people who hated me—they all lived in this town once. Now it's just another place.

I pull into Denny's and order a Grand Slam breakfast, amazed at how young the kids are in here, how obviously drunk and high and annoying they all are.

"SO, TELL ME ABOUT YOUR HEAD," my brother-in-law says, in his sports analyst voice. My real brother is drinking wine and sitting on a lawn chair. This is a Sunday family dinner, a throwback to the old days.

"It feels like it's splitting open," I say. Because of all the beer the night before, this is truer than ever.

"No, I mean what happened?"

"Don't even ask," Grandma says.

"It was just a slip," I say.

"You can say that again," Grandma says.

It was one of those freak chilly summer nights and I had nothing else to do, so I walked down to the factory where I used to wind transformers. I'm not an angry guy but the empty building was too much. I threw a few rocks at a few windows and then tried to climb up the building and get inside. I didn't make it.

"You were drunk, right?" my brother says. "Please tell me you were drunk."

I don't say anything, and for a while nobody else does either. We go through the ritual of a family dinner, but it breaks up sooner than it ever did back when my grandfather was alive.

I LIKE HENRY SCREW'S DOG. I like the fact that he has no name. It's just "dog," just like Grandma's dog is just "dog." It's a return to elemental forms. When I go over to cut his lawn, I take Grandma's dog to play with Henry Screw's dog and they mime-bark together. I can't tell if Screw's dog is mocking Grandma's dog or if it's a show of compassion. The whippet runs rings around the Shih Tzu. I put them both in the middle of the yard. After a while the Shih Tzu sinks down on the grass and follows the blurred shape of the whippet with its head. Its eyes leak and it looks wasted.

I put them both inside while I mow the lawn, and they jump against the window with every pass I make, their little dog noses and dog tongues making marks on the pane.

ON THE WAY BACK FROM THE VETS, we stop at a hot dog shack by the industrial river and watch sludge-colored water pass beneath us. The hot dog place is only busy on weekends now, when people who grew up in the town but moved away to safer towns come back for nostalgic foot-longs. Grandma's wearing a matching purple velour sweatsuit.

"This is it," she says. I don't know what she means so I don't say anything back.

"I'm selling the house," she continues.

"Why?"

"*You* see those people around there. *You* know what it's like. And it's not going to get any better."

"I haven't had any problems," I say.

"You also don't have any money. And there's no way I'd just *give* you the house. Drive me to bingo," she says.

I drop her off at the front door of the senior center.

"It's been nice having you around, though," she says when she gets out, like it's the last time she'll ever see me.

When I pick her up after an hour and a half her nose is red, her eyes water.

"Broke even," she says.

HENRY SCREW THROWS A BIRTHDAY PARTY for himself. Cars are parked up and down the street, but they're for the Kingdom Hall, which is having some kind of ceremony. At the party it's just me, Grandma, Henry, and the dogs. We drink beer. The stitches have dissolved into my scalp. The only problem I have now is an occasional headache. I sleep two or three hours a night. I'm thinking of looking for a job.

"How's it feel," Henry asks, "to have the hottest grand-mother in the world?"

"Did he ever race?" I ask, pointing at the whippet.

"They beat him like hell," Henry says. He puts on a party hat and blows a noisemaker that doesn't make noise. I wonder if he actually bought this stuff, or if it was just hanging around in his house. It's stuff a grandfather would just naturally have. I'm not sure if Henry is a grandfather, but it stands to follow.

People leave the Kingdom Hall slowly, in ones and twos. Me and Henry watch them.

"Let's dance, Henry," Grandma says.

They go inside and leave me alone. I have nothing to do. I just sit there with the dogs. Grandma's dog is asleep while Screw's dog keeps looking up at me, like he expects something. I give him a sip of my beer.

Then I pick the whippet up and walk around the fence. I hold him like protection as I walk into the Kingdom Hall. I've always wanted to know what happens in here. I've never had the guts to find out. If not now, then when? The "hall" is just a large, plain room full of folding chairs. There's nothing happening. About twenty people sitting on chairs in a corner of the room turn to look at me, but their expressions don't change. They look like people who have always been here. People who don't have a doubt in their heads.

I place the whippet down on the smooth, buffed wood floor. He starts circling the room, slowly at first but then faster and faster, his nails scrabbling on the wood. He's running away from something, I think. He's a blur. Round and round. The sound of his nails becomes one constant noise. The twenty people watch, staring, like they don't know what to make of us. I'm trying to put the big picture together, I want to tell them. Finally, the dog loses its footing, slams into the front door, and lays on its side with its tongue out, looking around.

The Animals of Gram Land

Everywhere we've lived, until now, has been full of other people. There was the apartment complex outside Atlanta where our neighbors were mostly old. There was the trailer park in Massachusetts—my favorite. I had friends; we played in the woods. Here no one is ever around. There's only flat land curling up a little at the end out the windows. There are animals out there, too, supposedly, though I haven't seen any yet. The emptiness can get to you, do things to you, make your bones sing with a low frequency.

We've moved in with my father's mother, who I'd never met before we came here. She's old old, wears wooly things, and looks at me out of a wrinkled head. She seems to have no inclination to get to know me, which is fine by me, I don't want to get to know her either. My father tells me to call her Gram, but when I call her Gram she ignores me. Maybe she's deaf, but I don't think so. She wanders around the house all the time. It must be tough to have a house on the edge of nothing where you're always alone and then to have three people move in, no matter how much you're supposed to love those three people.

She must forget we exist. We are ghosts to her.

One night I wake up, wander down the stairs, walk quietly to the bathroom, and see her standing by the back doors. Sliding glass doors looking out on the nothing. The moon, bright and full, makes the wrinkles on her head and neck stand out. Wearing her white wooly suit, she stands staring. When I look out I see movement near distant hills. I'm pretty sure it's a herd of something. Buffalo? Elk? How would I know?

I pee, go back to bed, and all I see in my mind is Gram standing there. She looks lonesome for the animals. Like she wants to join them. I picture her zipping the hood of the wooly suit up over her head. There are no eyeholes on the hood, just the silver strip of zipper running down the center of where her face would be. Frightening.

Another night I wake up and she's standing in the doorway looking in at me. It must be strange to have rooms you can't go into anymore in your own house, but there are tons of other rooms. This one doesn't seem special.

"Hi Gram."

"Marielle."

I'm surprised she knows my name.

"What are you doing?"

"I'm just looking in at you."

"What do you see?"

"I see you. Good night."

"Good night."

Her voice is ripped paper. Parchment or waxed paper. Beautiful but thin. I wonder if I'll sound like that when I'm old. I've never thought about being an old woman before, but now I do.

My father works in the basement, moving between three different computer monitors, following stocks, a stocks analyst. And my mother stays in their room reading the Bible with little fingers. She has always been small but seems to be shrinking even more since we moved here. I can tell Gram doesn't like her, which is fine by me; I don't like her either. I think of her as my stepmother even though she isn't.

It's not until we've been here a month that I go out and explore. It's daunting. So flat and empty. I walk a long ways from the house but don't seem to get any closer to the hills, so I walk back. I do that a few days: walk out, walk back, walk out, walk back. There's never been a child in the house. There are no other houses around with children. I have only the memory of my friends in Massachusetts to keep me company, and those are fading fast. Then they're gone.

We have conversations now and then, me and Gram, all like the one in my bedroom.

"What are you doing, Gram?"

"I'm standing, looking out the window."

"Is there anything out there?"

"There are all kinds of things out there. Can't you see?"

"I don't know."

I ask my father for a bike. It gets delivered the next day, a BMX bike with red rims and high handlebars. I learned to ride a bike in Massachusetts. All the kids at the trailer park had them.

I ride over the flat empty land toward the hills. For a long time they don't seem to get any closer. Then they do. The land becomes rockier. Crows circle above me, so many they kind of blot out the sun. I look back and see the house. It sits alone in the middle of land. I know there are three people inside, living three different lives, but it doesn't look like there's anyone back there.

I guess in a way I love each one of them in a different way.

Finally I get to the hills. There are tracks all over the place, from buffalo or elk. Maybe. There's scat. I find the skull of something near where trees start. It fits in my hand. I look into the woods. There's nothing to see but woods, yet it's still strange and wonderful.

Back at the house, I put the skull on a shelf in my room.

"I like that," Gram says, from the doorway.

"The skull?"

"Yes. I like that."

"I'm glad."

"Good night, Marielle."

"Good night, Gram."

That night I dream the land is animal-full. Hundreds of buffaloes. There are big birds, sandhill cranes, I guess. There are people, too, but not modern-day people.

Every day after that I ride my bike out to the hills.

Once I see a girl there who wears a white dress, but when I come closer she disappears.

At night sometimes I sit up with Gram. Every full moon, she stands by the back doors looking out.

"Aren't you going to look?" she asks me.

"Sure," I say.

I get up and stand next to her watching the herd of whatever-they-are in the distance. They move like a river. Maybe, I think, we'll stay here.

Lakes and Rivers

Thanks to Covid, they were sitting six feet apart in the parking lot, on folding chairs; maybe that was why it was hard for Haggett to pay attention to anything Tod Abrams said. Abrams was an ex-con in a black polo shirt, a local they were supposed to look up to. It was like old rags were flopping out of the man's mouth in place of words. Haggett didn't even know what the hell he was talking about, something about hitting rock bottom. Clean for seven days, he was already sick of hearing the same old shit, was pretty sure he wasn't going to make it very long this time—probably not even longer than last time, when he'd made it fourteen days, two weeks of pure hell. Got his fourteen day keychain then went out and got fucked up, a night of oxy and Jack with his old buddy Stiv. They'd gone to the river like they did when they were teenagers. Already he was sick of hearing about the twelve steps, sick of the constant refrain that they couldn't do it by themselves, that they needed to give up all illusion of control and hand their lives over to the program, to their sponsor, to their "higher power." Whatever.

Haggett planned to maintain control over his own life, thank you very much.

When they did the keychain ceremony, Haggett went up to get his seven day keychain—he was the first to stand, the person who'd been clean the shortest amount of time, and they all cheered for him. He couldn't deny that it felt good to get that kind of support. These people actually cared about him, at least for these couple seconds.

It was only when the meeting was almost over that he noticed Karly, a girl he'd gone to high school with, sitting on her own metal folding chair. Back then she'd been smart as hell, so smart she made everyone else feel stupid, college bound, not a fuckup like him, and yet... here she was. Somehow she had become just another fuckup, like him. Haggett had seen a picture of her on Instagram, wearing a shirt that tied near her navel. She'd had a dagger tattooed, point down, on her breastbone, probably ten inches long. He remembered the way she'd stared into the camera, this look on her face. Don't fuck with me, that look said. And/or I have seen some shit. Her face still held some of the innocence of her high school face. He could see the little kid she'd been in her face still, the kid who wanted so badly to do the right thing. You could tell that at one time she'd done everything she was supposed to do, had expected her life to follow an easy, upward trajectory, high school to college to career to… whatever came next. Family. Settling down, somewhere far from Cumberland. Sometimes those were the people who fell hardest, the ones who had it all figured out. At least Haggett had never thought he had it all figured out. There were benefits to being the perpetual fuckup.

Now, in the parking lot on the edge of the historical section of town, Karly was wearing gray sweatpants and an oversized white tee, wet hair plastered to her scalp like she'd just showered. Her bare feet were tucked underneath her. A brief image flared in his mind: he imagined going over, kneeling in front of her, taking her bare feet in his hands and just holding them, but how fucked up would that be? He had no idea why he wanted to do it. He didn't have a fetish or anything.

When the meeting was over, the crowd broke up slowly, the way they always did, getting into small groups to talk, some of them maintaining the six feet distance, most not giving a shit now that the meeting was over, little clots of people talking about whatever they had to talk about. Grandkids, some of them. Their jobs or, more likely, their lack of jobs. Sports. The weather; it was summer but not for long. Haggett had two goals: one, to escape from his sponsor, a woman named Joanie who'd worked at a factory all her life before being laid off and getting hooked on oxy (the usual story: pain management, a lapsed prescription, a turn to street drugs), and two, to talk to Karly. He saw Joanie's gray head swiveling like a meerkat, ready to track him down and give him some great advice about how to move from step one to step two, ready to congratulate him on his new keychain, and he darted down the alley after his old classmate.

He caught up to her on the corner of Mechanic Street.

"Hey," he said.

"Hey." She didn't look at him, clearly not in the mood to talk. The word was not really a word but an angry syllable that actually said "fuck off."

"Haggett."

"I know."

"Yeah." He wiped his hands on his jeans. "I didn't know you were in the program."

"I am."

And then she slipped down an alley a few yards up, on the other side of Mechanic Street. She didn't want to be bothered, so he let her go, wasn't going to hound her. Wasn't that kind of guy.

"See you around," he called after her. She lifted her hand behind her head. Hard to tell whether she was giving him the finger or not. He didn't blame her, if she was. He was sure she had to deal with assholes all the time. Guys trying to get inside those sweatpants. He imagined it for a second:

her smooth skin, the curve of her lower back, then pulled himself up quick. It didn't do any good to think about shit like that.

He got into his old Corolla, with its worn paint job that had once been light blue and the dent on the side from where he'd driven into he-didn't-remember-what one night when he was fucked up, a deer probably, and drove back to his apartment on Haigh Street, on the west side. His neighborhood was a dense triangle of old houses built in the early twentieth century, wedged between busy roads, all the houses falling apart, siding giving way to brick, stone giving way to siding, clapboard and asbestos, windows rotting, old porches, weird things in windows, like porcelain poodles.

There were about a dozen churches in his neighborhood, and about a hundred kids who roamed the streets in different packs, heads shaved for the summer, arms bare, boys and girls indistinguishable. Some of them were barely ten years old and had tattoos on their forearms. Fake, probably. Haggett had been one of those kids once, understood their mix of innocence and experience, knew they were all dangerous, and at the same time they were all just kids. Cats and dogs wandered the streets. He drove down the little alley behind the house and parked in the yard beside two overflowing trash cans.

It felt like he'd been away for years.

Tetley, the obese dude who lived on the first floor with three pitbulls, sat on the back deck, the dogs barking like assholes inside the apartment behind him. He glanced up when Haggett passed but didn't make any show of recognition. Whatever. He thought Haggett was a fuckup and a druggie. Which, guess what, asshole? You are absolutely right. But it doesn't make me any less human than you.

Haggett had lived on the second floor of the house for two years. He was only a month behind on rent now, thanks to his recent job at the casino complex. Groundskeeper for the golf course, mostly, though he did other things as needed: janitorial work in the pro shop, sometimes security on the casino floor when they were shorthanded. If an opening came up he was going to apply for it. He liked standing there having some semblance of authority, like a little cop. He didn't think he would like it, but it turned out....

He started up his old HP laptop, which weighed about fifteen pounds, and got onto Tetley's Wi-Fi network (Pittie19) then scrolled to Karly's Instagram page. Had to. Felt that familiar need, like whatever was crawling in his bones had seeped out into his blood. And there it was, the pic of her with her dagger tattoo. It got more likes than any of her other pics, probably from pervs who didn't even know her. There was something about the picture. Something about her eyes. Do not fuck with me, but, also, I'm in need of love and attention. She looked like a hurt dog. She probably had a fucked up life story, had experienced abuse in her past. Most women had. It was sad. He scrolled down her feed and found a picture of her bartending at one of the restaurants in the casino complex, the Cuban-themed place. No surprise there—there weren't many jobs in the area; half the employed people he knew worked at the casino complex—though he was a little surprised she was a bartender. She didn't seem social enough. He couldn't imagine her spending shifts talking to people. Though what the hell did he know?

It was getting dark, about seven thirty, but he didn't turn on any lights, didn't let himself log on to his usual porn sites, fuq.com or Pornhub, didn't do anything but close the laptop, sit there and watch the rooms get darker, all his shit becoming indistinguishable and lumpy. The couch, his old acoustic guitar, the amp he'd been holding for Holden for years but which was basically his now, a Marshall he couldn't play at even the lowest volume because Tetley would go nuts.

Yeah, right. Like he wasn't going to start using again. Like he wasn't going to go out and get fucked up. Like he wasn't going to keep searching for rock bottom until he found it.

WHEN HE WAS AT WORK NOW he felt like he could bump into Karly at any second, but it was going to be fall soon and there was plenty to do at the course, so he didn't think about it. His favorite job, aside from security, was to walk along the edge of the golf course picking shit up with one of those long poking sticks. The course had to be kept pristine for the rich assholes who came to vomit their money here. Haggett saw them walking the course in polo shirts that always looked new, as if they ripped open a new one every day they played a game.

There wasn't much to worry about around the edge of three quarters of the course, but along the edge where the course backed onto 81 there was always plenty of trash, fast food containers, used rubbers, water bottles full of piss, you name it. Dirty diapers, even. Used needles. It was amazing what made its way onto the roadside. Once, he'd found a fetus. He was pretty sure it was a deer fetus, but he was no biologist. He'd picked it up with an old plastic bag from Shoppers, trying not to feel the thing through the thin plastic. He carried big black plastic bags with him, and on most days he'd fill up one of them. After the weekend, it would be two or three. He found satisfaction in finishing the job, looking back and seeing the clean greenery, knowing he'd accomplished something. It was a feeling he'd always loved, even as a kid, when he'd liked to do stupid shit like rake leaves and help his father mow lawns for his landscaping business. He tried not to think about the fact that the second he turned his back some asshole would throw another bottle out his window on 81.

The whole casino complex felt like a replica of the real world, like what God would make if he'd only ever heard of nature. It had been carved out of the side of the mountain, and all the grounds were perfectly maintained, by a couple people who knew what they were doing supported by a small army of people who had no clue and just did whatever those smarter people told them to. It was like people, vacationers, rich fucks, wanted something that looked like wild nature, but not really. Give them something that smelled like the wilderness but wasn't the wilderness. Let them think they were really living.

Two mornings after he saw Karly at the meeting, into his ninth day clean, Haggett was on the course raking a sandtrap early in the morning when he looked over at a group of men on the ninth hole. It was barely dawn, but there they were, a bunch of assholes in polo shirts, shorts, and stupid golf shoes. They were just getting out of a couple golf carts. He zeroed in on one of them because he was about three times the size of the others, reminded him of Tetley. The others were slim and fit and had that look about them, like they had important things to do and they took even their leisure more seriously than other people.

Haggett had no idea what drew his attention to them. There were groups like that everywhere he looked. He watched the fat man line up his putt, looking down, then looking toward the hole. He waggled his ass for comedic effect, and the men around him laughed, and then it happened: the dude just... keeled over. There was no clutching the chest, no indication that anything was wrong. He was just standing there one second, and then he went over, his body impacting the ground, sending shockwaves through the course. A 4.0 on the Richter Scale.

The men didn't panic. One of them was on his phone within seconds, while the others crouched around the fat man. Haggett watched, wondering if he should walk over and act as a representative of the casino. Fuck that.

He stood watching the whole thing, watched them try to resuscitate the fat dude, giving him mouth to mouth, watched the ambulance arrive, driving on the surface road so they didn't mess up the course, throwing red lights across the greens, the EMTs jogging over. They knelt for a long time, pushing at the man's chest, using those paddles. Haggett could hear the paddles when they discharged electricity into the dude's body. *Zap.* It was all for nothing. *Zap.* They tried and tried again, but even from where Haggett stood he could tell it was useless. *Zap zap.* Finally they struggled to get the fattie onto a stretcher. His fat hung over the edges. It was obvious the dude was dead. No more golf for him. No more fine dining. No more captaining of industry.

There is a life lesson in this, Haggett, he told himself. He was pretty sure the life lesson wasn't that he should stop wasting his time and go out and get fucked up while he still could, but that was definitely one interpretation.

HE TOOK A SHOWER IN ONE of the locker room stalls and dressed in jeans, a plain black t-shirt and work boots. In the mirror he saw need burrowing into his eyes, like two dark holes in his face. He had no idea whether he was good looking or ugly. Somewhere in between, probably, like everyone else. He had short hair and regular features. Some girls told him he was good looking, but only when they wanted something from him. He did okay, but he wasn't a player like Stiv, who could get laid whenever he wanted, or Holden, who, because he was in a band and had long hair.... Haggett brushed his teeth, narrowed his eyes at himself, like he was going to give himself a pep talk, left the bathroom.

The casino was popping. It was Friday, late afternoon, and it was only going to get busier from here. Three years old, the place still had the new smell to it. The walls were dark brown, and it was like they were inside a huge cave, only that cave had a bunch of slot machines inside it making a crazy electronic jangle. Everyone had to wear a mask and keep six feet apart, and it was a little freaky to see so many people but not to see their mouths. Directional arrows on the floors told people where to go. Haggett could not get used to the arrows or the masks. He tried to read emotions in the faces, but the faces of winners and losers were identical. Half the people wore light blue disposable masks, the other half wore different kinds of masks, fashion masks or some shit. He saw a black couple, both wearing Black Lives Matter masks—which seemed pretty ballsy. Some older women wore leopard print masks. A bunch of people had black masks.

Haggett usually didn't walk through the casino after work because he didn't like the feeling of desperation here. It was too familiar. (And now that it was payday… how was he supposed to *stop* himself from procuring something? He was into oxy, mostly, but any opiate would do. His blood salivated in his veins, like little greedy creatures reaching out little greedy hands.) He wondered how gambling was any better than getting fucked up on oxy or heroin. Drug users got a bad rap, but every single person in this country was an addict, if you asked Haggett. Some of their vices became civic duty, but that didn't mean they weren't vices. The need to gamble, blow money, suck the cocks of the corporate gods. Shopping was seen as better than shooting up, but it was the same thing.

At the entrance to the Cuban-themed restaurant, he had his temperature taken—a regular occurrence nowadays—and was led to a seat at the bar. The place had cheesy Cuban-style decorations. The trunk and backfins of an old Ford. A fake rocket. Communist symbols everywhere. The lighting was dark, red. The two stools on either side of him at the bar were blocked off and plexiglass made a kind of booth for him and him alone. It was surreal. Seated, he took his mask off and breathed easier. He was relieved to see Karly walking toward him from across the bar. Couldn't tell, since she wore a black mask, what she was thinking, or if she even recognized him.

"Hey," he said.

She jerked her head up at him. She wore a green sleeveless tee and black jeans and he felt a grumbling in his throat. He had an image of kissing her with her mask on, his tongue poking out to meet the walled resistance of cotton.

"Uh, Corona, I guess," he smiled, a joke. She put the beer in front of him and left him alone. He watched her work. She was one of those kinds of bartenders, the ones who would barely talk to you. The bitchy/asshole bartenders. There was a certain appeal to that. It made people try harder, he guessed. Everyone felt like they deserved to be treated like shit anyway. Whenever she passed behind the bar, he looked at her, tried to get her to come over, but she never did, and when he finished the beer he paid for it and walked out.

Fuck it. It wasn't worth it. None of it was worth it.

He went home, jerked off, sat on his couch watching a *Fast and Furious* movie he'd accidentally bought once on his Xfinity account and seen a dozen times already. He kept the lights off, still tasting that one beer from the bar, thinking about Karly, thinking about going out and giving some kid his money, thinking about getting fucked up, thinking about how stupid and sad his life had become, thinking about his father, who'd died when he was fifteen and thrown his whole life off course. Car crash. He'd been drunk at the time, because that was his vice.

Haggett thought of his mother, living with some asshole in a trailer across town. He wished life were more like stories, or movies, wished something would happen to push him forward, out of this hole he was in. Thought about killing himself. If he had a gun he'd probably put the barrel in his mouth and sit there thinking about it, rolling the possibilities over in his head. Maybe spin the barrel. He felt pretty shitty, but it still wasn't rock bottom.

THE NEXT MORNING HE WALKED to the Rock of Ages Christian Nightclub and Diner, on the other side of the tracks. Under the tracks, he had to walk down old cement stairs built into the side of the road, beside a narrow tunnel where cars passed right beside him, everything old and rusty and rotten. Brick and stone. He smelled coal in the air. Felt grit on his skin. It was cooler than it had been, his arms turning gooseflesh.

He didn't usually go out to breakfast, but he had to keep himself occupied somehow. Life was just different ways of passing time. He had money in his pocket, wasn't scheduled to work that day, and the only way he wasn't going to get fucked up was to fill those hours.

The Rock of Ages had never been a nightclub, but there was a bar with no bottles behind it lining one of the walls. The ceiling was hanging tile, the floors linoleum. It looked like an Elk's Hall, and Walter, the dude who owned the place, reinforced that feeling. He sat on a stool behind the bar with his gray beard and long gray hair, in his black tee with the MIA logo, arms crossed on his chest. He always wore the same tee. Or maybe he had dozens of them.

Walter nodded at Haggett when he walked in.

Along with a few couples, there were two large groups in the big room—one group of old fucks wearing windbreakers and button-ups near the back, another group of volunteer firemen clustered around a table in the exact middle of the restaurant. He recognized all of them. Guys from town. Guys from school. Half were about his age, some were younger, some older, but they were all built on the same basic plan. A lot of mustaches and beer bellies. They had the well-fed look of domesticated animals. Some of them called out to him, and he nodded, raised his hand.

He sat in a booth near the front, as far away from anyone as he could without seeming rude, and when Jenny Olds came over, wearing a flowered mask and a pink t-shirt, he nodded at her.

"Hey, Haggett. Haven't seen you in a while. How's it hanging?"

"Oh, you know."

"You look good. Real good."

He shrugged. "Coffee," he said.

Jenny had been his girlfriend for almost his entire sophomore year of high school. He hated to think of how he'd treated her. He hadn't treated her well—like shit, actually—but she hadn't minded. He'd neglected her, ignored her, never gave her anything for her birthday or holidays. Abandoned her all the time so he could play video games or jam with his buddies. She had expected to be treated like shit.

Now he regretted it. It was Jenny who'd helped him through that dark period after his father died. He hated to remember, but he couldn't help but remember her holding him while he sobbed on his bed, her hands on his back, her words a reassuring murmur. She was the only one in the world who'd ever seen him like that. Not even his mother had seen him like that. And now they were basically strangers.

Life was weird.

He thought about how much he hated this town. He didn't hate the people in it, not anymore, but he hated the town and what it did to people, how it dulled them. It was like that thing that punched cows in the head and made them dumb and docile. That was Cumberland.

He watched Jenny Olds walk around the diner, laughing with people, men especially. She was skinny, had no curves. The men didn't flirt with her, exactly, because it was a Christian diner, the walls covered with pictures of Jesus Christ and folded hands in prayer, a flag of Israel and a POW flag hanging side by side behind the bar, other decorations for the coming fall already hanging up, pumpkins and shit, but they came awful close to flirting with her.

He wondered if Jenny Olds was happy with her life, if this was it for her. He noticed the ring on her finger. Figured she'd be pregnant before long, if she wasn't already. Popping babies out one after the other, more cows for the cowpuncher.

HE FOUND HIMSELF TURNING right once he was out of the Rock of Ages, his gut full of sausage and pancakes and eggs, a meal like he hadn't eaten in years. When he was using, he only ate enough to sustain. Didn't savor anything. Now he felt full and tired. All he wanted to do was lay down and take a nap, but he found himself turning in the opposite direction from his apartment anyway. The day had warmed, but there was a bite of fall in the air, and it made him feel good to be alive, need or no need. Cars passed on the busy road, pushing air against him. It was good to have something to push against.

He figured he could just keep walking, didn't have to actually stop. Walking cleared his mind. Sometimes he wished he didn't think at all, wished there was nothing in his head but echoing space, but he found himself worrying about the future way too often, worrying about the "meaning of life," or some shit. As if he was ever going to figure it out. Nobody figured it out.

He knew exactly where he was going, but he didn't really plan it. If he let himself think about it too much he'd probably turn around, go back to his place and try to figure out how to spend the hours without going out and getting fucked up. Or, more likely, he would have just gone and done it. Why keep waiting on the inevitable?

She was sitting out in what counted as a yard of the trailer, smoking. He could feel the moment she spotted him coming. She had big hair ("quarantine hair" people called it) and long nails, and the cigarette between her fingers had a long ash. She'd pulled a thick gray cardigan around her shoulders, and for the first time he noticed how old she was, realized, suddenly, that she was going to die. Not sometime in the distant future, but within twenty years, at most. Death was stamped on her face.

He was relieved she was outside, that he didn't have to knock on the door. Maybe he could get away without having to see that asshole Frank at all.

"The return of the prodigal son," she called out as he approached.

"I don't even know what that means."

"Neither do I, to be honest." She ashed the cigarette and smiled at him.

It was weird the way people changed. She was a completely different person than the person who'd raised him. Once his father had died, the transformation had begun. It had been quick and brutal. Her fingernails grew, she started smoking, stains on her teeth, stains on her fingers. She dried up, lost twenty pounds. He didn't blame her; how could he? Some things are beyond people's capabilities. She hadn't started using, the way he had, but she had become desperate, embarrassing, dressing up, going out to bars, bringing home random men—some of them had been dicks to him, most had ignored him, one or two, the worst, tried to act like his friend. She had pretended to have a new lease on life, while he sobbed on his bed with Jenny Olds. That was not a time period he wanted to remember.

He got the lawn chair leaning against the trailer behind her and lined it up next to her.

They sat, watching cars and trucks. Across the road was the old glass factory that hadn't been operational for fifteen years, a complex of low buildings, the power lines above it thick. He wondered why they didn't demolish the place, make it a park or something. When he was a teenager he'd broken in once, looking for windows to smash. They were all smashed already.

"Well," she said, after a while. "Are you going to ask for money?"

"No."

He hunched forward. It had been a stupid idea, coming here.

"Find a job yet?" he asked.

"Not yet."

"They're hiring at the casino."

"Yeah."

She lit another cigarette. He wondered if she remembered anything from when he was growing up. It wasn't like they'd been an ideal family. They had struggled. They fought—her and his father, him and her, him and his father, sometimes all of them at the same time. But there had been good times, too. Playing Monopoly late into the night. Going places. Lakes and rivers. He remembered playing video games with his father, sitting on the floor shoulder to shoulder with their backs against the couch.

"I'm clean," he said.

"Yeah? How long?"

"Eight days?" he shrugged. "Nine."

"Good for you, Lucas."

He could feel her looking at him, waiting for him to turn toward her, so he did.

"I'm proud of you," she said.

He nodded. "I better go."

"Okay. Thanks for stopping by."

He nodded again, got up, walked away. When he was about a hundred yards away he turned back. She was looking in the other direction, smoking her cigarette. She would sit there for hours, watching cars and trucks pass.

HE SAW THE EVENT ANNOUNCEMENT on Facebook, which he barely went on anymore: Holden's band was playing at the brewery outside town. The 1812. He'd been there only once before. It was where locals with jobs and money and some of the younger people in town went if they didn't go to the brewery in town. By that point in the day, he felt like smashing shit. Tearing things off the wall. Breaking something. This jumble of need in his veins. He just wanted to get fucked up and forget everything. His anger came in waves like this. It was never easy, never completely gone from him, but at five p.m. it was almost insane. No way could he hold out much longer. Need ran behind his eyeballs and under his skin.

It was stupid to even pretend. He sat on the edge of his couch, the TV playing a rerun of *The Fugitive*, bouncing a little, every second a conscious decision not to bound up, run outside and score something, anything. He'd even do meth at this point, something he'd told himself he'd never do. One of those stupid rules that don't make sense. I'll shoot up some horse, but I draw the line at meth. He went into the kitchen and thought about making coffee, started making coffee, the last thing he needed was coffee.

He went out, got into his Corolla and drove around, a few dozen miles up 81, over the hills, passing big trucks on the inclines. He drove past the casino complex, looking at the edge of the golf course where he'd picked shit up the day before, noticing all the shit that was there again, out all the way to 70, where he got off the highway then turned back around. He listened to classic rock as he drove. They were playing all of Van Halen's *Diver Down*—"Where Have all the Good Times Gone"—how appropriate—and he cranked it up, then he took the back roads and got a little lost, but he couldn't really get lost because he'd lived in western Maryland all his life and all roads he didn't know eventually led to roads he did.

Finally he pulled into the parking lot of the 1812 Brewery, out in the middle of nowhere. It was about 6:30 and the place was already filling up. The lot was a big field, the brewery itself inside an old barn up the hill. They had fixed it up, on the cheap. There was a big concrete slab outside the barn with picnic tables, a stage where they had live bands, sometimes halfway decent bands from out of state but usually local talent, like Holden's band, the George Jennings Experiment. There was no one named George Jennings. They had mixed Waylon Jennings and George Jones together. They played more rock than country, but no one cared what they were called.

It was a cool night and people lined up by the window where you ordered, most of them wearing masks, ordering IPLs and IPAs, Imperials and Hazies, whatever they were called. Haggett didn't know beer, didn't care, felt alone and conspicuous, like everyone was looking at him wondering what he was doing there alone. Most of the people looked brushed up. Half of them were probably young parents having someone babysit their kids back home. There were a few college age groups. A small group of dudes who were squat and awkward wearing ironic t-shirts. Jesus, it was like high school.

He ordered a pilsner and sat in one of the metal chairs at the edge of the concrete patio looking around, not really scoping out the women but kind of. He figured he'd have one beer then leave. He'd let Holden know he was there, watch a song or two, then bail. If this was the way normal people spent their time, he wanted no part of it.

He texted Stiv, letting him know where he was, but got no response. Stiv was probably out getting laid or getting fucked up. Stiv could use and maintain at the same time. Haggett's twelve step program had told him to break contact with people like Stiv, that they were exactly who he should avoid. He was supposed to abandon the only two friends he had, just because they got fucked up once in a while. That might be other people, but that wasn't Haggett.

He felt like he wasn't really there, and he wound up drinking the beer too fast and getting another one. Finally he caught up with Holden. It was getting dark and Holden was heading to the stage, Les Paul tucked under his arm. They stood together for a couple seconds. "What's going on, Haggett?" Holden said.

"Yeah, what's up?"

"You know how it is. Thanks for coming."

And then he was on stage and Haggett was alone again.

THREE BEERS IN? FOUR? He was a few in, barely listening to the band, which sounded like they weren't really into it, when he spotted Karly from a distance, standing with a dude who looked ten years older than her. He had black hair combed straight back, wore a short-sleeve button-up shirt that was too tight, showing off his tatts and impressive biceps. *Fuck me. What the fuck am I doing?*

Haggett was tempted to leave, go and score and get fucked up. The thought of laying on his couch with heroin flowing through his veins, opening everything up—hosanna hosanna—was about the best thought he'd ever had. A primo plan. What was the point of any of this? The band was playing "Sweet Home Alabama," for god's sake, and women in their thirties and forties, wearing jeans and high heels, were dancing in that swaying way drunk middle-aged women danced at weddings.

He watched them from a distance get their beers, watched him lead her to a table at the opposite corner of the patio, watched them talking. She leaned toward him while she took off her black mask. God, what was he thinking? She was out of his league. The dude was handsome, with a face like a rock. His arms. His tatts. Whatever.

He ignored them and sat watching Holden lean into a solo. They used to jam together, but Haggett had never been good enough. He should have taken up the bass or something, because he didn't have the chops to make it as a guitarist. But what did it matter? Holden was the best musician he'd ever known, and he was stuck here in Cumberland anyway. Was never going to get out and get a record deal. He recorded shit on his computer, and even though some of it was okay, it wasn't good enough to get airplay or any attention. All the young people were into hip-hop now, making beats or whatever. There were probably millions of dudes like Holden, almost but not quite good enough. That was life for most people.

AND THEN SHE WAS CROUCHING BESIDE HIM, pulling at his arm, rousing him from his stupor. Karly.

"Get me out of here," she said.

And he was standing up, more than a little drunk, letting her lead him away from the patio, into the darkness behind the barn. She pulled his arm. She wore fancy hiking boots and jeans and she moved quickly through the dark, holding his arm and laughing.

"What's happening?" he said, laughing with her.

"Shhhh."

And then they were in his Corolla, and she was saying "go, go, go," and leaning down in the passenger seat, and he was driving out onto the backroads again. He was drunk but not drunk drunk. He'd driven in far worse condition dozens of times. Still, he had to be careful, had to follow that yellow line, which sometimes wasn't there. Cops loved to pull people over out here.

"God, that motherfucker would *not* stop talking," she said.

He nodded, turned on the radio. He was sick of classic rock, but it was the safest choice. If he'd been sober he would have been nervous as hell. As it was he heard his heart thudding underneath the ocean of his drunkenness. He could smell her. Shampoo? Beer? A little edge of sweat?

The roads were dark, no streetlights, and each curve took him by surprise.

"I want to get fucked up so fucking bad," he said, and he heard sadness in his voice, an honesty he didn't usually hear.

"I hear you. So do I."

She kind of curled on the passenger's seat, putting her boots on the seat, bit at her fingernail.

"Let's go to the river," she said.

"Are you holding?"

"No. Let's go to the river."

He nodded, tried to concentrate on the road, figure out where the hell he was, Supertramp playing loud on the radio, need running along his veins like a razor. *Goodbye, Mary. Goodbye, Jane.* The song was probably about drugs. Most songs from the 70s were.

"How do people do it?" he said.

"It beats the fuck out of me."

And then they were parked by the side of the road, sitting in the car letting their eyes adjust to the darkness. He remembered her from high school, when she had seemed so perfect. He should have known better.

"Let's go," she said.

And he had to follow her through the woods. She moved quickly, too quickly. He was drunk and had to trust himself not to bash into branches.

"Come on, come on, come on," she said. There was no moon. He wondered… he wondered if he could follow her forever, if she could just keep leading him deeper into the dark woods, if they would get lost. He didn't want them to stop. He knew they would stop eventually—they would come to the river a few hundred yards away—but he didn't want to get to that moment yet. He wanted to keep following her through the woods, the edge of everything dulled, his heart beating, chasing her but not chasing her.

American Animism

When Danny went over to what used to be his old house for her 11th birthday party, Haydn stayed in bed most of the night. Haydn was dying. Stage two. Leukemia. It was a tragedy. That was all anyone could say about it, if they said anything.

Her friends helped her down the hallway to the kitchen when the cake came out. They warbled, pretending it was a normal birthday. Then helped her blow out the candles, the two friends she'd had for years. Haydn looked frail, like a wraith. Danny had to look away so he didn't cry. When he looked at her face he could see features of his own face, his mother's face. The narrow nose, the tapered chin.

The Friday after her birthday, she slept at his place because his ex-wife had a date. She hadn't slept at his place since his second wife Allie had had Tommy, his son. Even before the leukemia, he'd been afraid he would mess her up somehow, that she would think he didn't love her as much as he loved his new child (which was not true).

Haydn doted on her little half-brother. Danny felt weird putting them in the same room together, as if the leukemia might be contagious, which was stupid, but he moved in a cot and made a nest for her. They ate pizza and played games, him and Haydn and Allie. They took turns caring for the baby. It felt almost normal, like a family. They put the baby down and watched *Whale Wars* for a while.

Overnight there was a storm, and in the early morning he found himself awake with Haydn, dressed in a thick hoodie and sweatpants and looking small small, in the kitchen listening to the wind die down.

"Let's go," he whispered, in the quiet of the house.

Haydn nodded, and they headed outside.

They used to do this often together, when Haydn was a little girl—go to the beach following storms to see if any lobster traps had washed up, with lobsters trapped inside. It was a kind of poaching, he supposed, though it didn't feel like it.

On the island he parked near a cove only locals knew about. The dawn was purple. Haydn seemed stronger than she'd been the week before, but they walked slowly so she didn't overexert herself. She kept her hands in the pocket of her sweatshirt, shuffled in Uggs. He could see only the profile of her face inside the hood.

A bead of sunrise appeared bloodred in the distant sky.

They didn't say anything. Just walked the beach remembering. Haydn had always been an imaginative child. Anything she found on the beach would come alive. Rocks, shells, the dried bodies of horseshoe crabs. She'd held them in her hand and made them talk. They'd found hermit crabs and watched them for what felt like hours. They'd come here to see the seals in the cove, and she'd told him stories about selkies. To her, everything was alive.

They found two lobsters tangled in the broken slats of a lobster trap, still alive. They were both beautiful and otherworldly, and he held one in each hand as they slowly walked the beach.

Later, before he took her back to her mother's, before he said goodbye to her for another few days, days that would feel long and perilous, they stood together around the kitchen table. Water boiled inside a huge speckled pot on the stove. The two black segmented bodies of the lobsters crawled on the kitchen table. Tommy, in Haydn's arms, watched them with wide eyes, half-afraid, confronting the elemental.

Danny wondered what the lobsters were thinking.

Wolf Haven

The wolves ranged behind the chain link fence that summer. They seemed unsettled. Maybe it was just his imagination, but they seemed unsure of the hierarchy in the pack. There was definitely a contest among the males as to who was the alpha, but the alpha female was set. It was clearly Sika. Because they were not in the wild, Sika was more or less the alpha of the whole pack, which had only about three acres of rocky Massachusetts woods to roam.

Visitors came, and he stood in front of the chain link fence talking about wolves in general and these gray wolves in particular. The kids who came loved that they had names. They loved the white female, Snowball, who was actually the omega female of the pack but was the most striking. Some kids clutched stuffed wolves to their chests. He could relate. He had been one of those weird little kids once, too, obsessed with all animals. He still was, to some degree, but now he was sixteen years old and his life felt unsettled. There was the future, college and all that, and there was Teresa, his mother's new woman, who had moved in to Wolf Haven with them. Teresa was a current accountant and a former college basketball player, had made it to the Final Four, and she was strong and loud, but she did not like the wolves, and she liked the halfbreeds they kept closer to the house even less. She refused to go back into the enclosures. She complained about how much time his mother spent with the animals. Why did she want to be with his mother, whose whole life was the wolves, anyway, he wondered?

As the summer wore on the wolves got closer and closer to the chain link fence, until they were pressing their flanks against it and looking up at him as he talked to the crowds assembled on the wooden observation platforms. They seemed to expect something from him. He wasn't afraid of them. He had basically grown up with them—his mother was always warning him to respect their wild natures more than he did. They were not pets, she made clear. This was a sanctuary and they were, and had to remain, to the extent it was possible, wild. Still, sometimes at night he looked out his window, and he would see them in the moonlight moving between the trees, and he would think either that he was one of them or that they "belonged" to him. Less often now than he used to. There was Sika, Charles, Sima, Moonlight, Wally, Tuna, Turkey, Snowball. He'd named most of them when he was a kid. Two years earlier Sam, one of the oldest members of the pack, had died and the pack had mourned his death. He still missed Sam.

The halfbreeds, who had a much smaller enclosure, seemed to be closer to pets, but they were even more dangerous than the wolves, because they had both the nature of domestic animals and the nature of wild animals. It was best to not even name them, though some of them had come with names like Killer and Sarge. They'd had to put several of them down because they couldn't be socialized either to humans or to each other. Someone always assumed it would be cool to own a half-wolf. They had stopped rescuing halfbreeds, and the three that remained would be the last. They attacked any time anyone approached their enclosure, even with food. He thought it was cruel to keep them there where they could hear the wolves howling (during every tour they induced the pack to howl; it was the highlight of the program).

He and his mother alternated giving the tours and working in the gift shop. Teresa did not refuse to help; she was never asked. He would see her in the living quarters behind the gift shop in the morning, wearing a red robe. He would wonder how she found a robe that could cover the generous expanse of her body. She seemed gargantuan to him, but also, and more worryingly, attractive. She was only five years younger than his mother but seemed closer to his age than to hers. She was careless with her body, as if her sexual preference precluded attraction on his part. Her smell, which seemed to change subtly day by day, if not hour by hour, induced something in him he refused to name, a free-ranging desire that moved through his body and blood. He hated her for many reasons—for not liking the wolves, for making him feel the way he did, for taking his mother's attention away from him. Not that he wanted his mother's attention, or would ever admit that he did, not at his age. It was all so complicated.

That was also the summer he was discovering drugs and studying for his driver's license test. He smoked joints and bowls with his friends as they drove through the dark Massachusetts nights. They got wasted regularly, laid around in someone's room. Mark, his best friend, had a barn behind his house where they kept guitars and old busted furniture, and they'd sit in wing-backed chairs getting high and listening to a boombox play the music of their parents' generation—Crosby, Stills and Nash, Simon and Garfunkel, Pink Floyd—while the light purpled out the open sliding doors. Animals, or maybe just the ghosts of animals, shuffled in dark corners while they talked. He told Mark about his hatred for Teresa but never his desire.

The summer was long, hot, and strange. He felt himself changing inside his head, as if his brain were the seed of a nut. Was he becoming more himself? Or less? Was he becoming someone completely new? It was difficult to tell. He read Kafka and Toni Morrison and gave tours and got high and masturbated trying not to picture his mother's new woman. Their relationship was serious, and someday, maybe, she could become his stepmother, in fact if not by law. He wrote bad poetry and got his driver's license. His mother drove him to the DMV. She was a stout woman with a helmet of short curly hair. She sang along to Joni Mitchell in the car. *They paved paradise and put up a parking lot.* They'd been alone together ever since his father left them. She started Wolf Haven when he was five years old. He didn't normally think of her as a strong, courageous woman, but for a second while she was driving him to the DMV he realized that that was exactly who she was.

Summer ended and school started again. He couldn't stand it. He'd been bullied throughout middle school because of his high voice, which hadn't changed when other boys' voices did, and for his innocence, his boyish face, his general pacifism, his love for animals, his weird broken family. He'd been shoved against and sometimes into lockers. Once he'd been locked in a stairwell with two bigger boys who took turns punching him in the stomach. When he went down, curling like a pillbug, they kicked his head until everything rang. He was black and blue afterwards and his head continued to ring for weeks. Permanent damage? Perhaps. In high school he found his people, fellow outcasts who did drugs in a time period in which that was relatively unusual. Most of his "peers" drank, but he and his friends experimented with hallucinogens, mostly. They dropped whatever was being passed off as acid in those days, and they lost their goddamned minds. They dreamed about taking peyote and ayahuasca. They read Kerouac and Burroughs. The school day was a round of classes he didn't care about and social interactions he wanted to merely survive. There were popular kids who wore polo shirts and boat shoes, and there were "heads," who wore denim jackets and boots. He and his three friends didn't fit in with any of them. They all wanted it just to end.

During the fall he continued to give tours, but there were fewer now, one on Saturday, one on Sunday. He found himself looking at the faces of the people he was giving tours to, searching for a girl. For a while he'd had a strange, secret feeling that someday he would meet the perfect girl for him, his soulmate. Why not here? They would look at each other, recognize each other, and that would be it. He was horny, of course, but he also wanted the kind of romantic love he saw in old movies—which the three of them watched together sometimes at night. *Casablanca* and *Double Indemnity*. He hated hated hated the way his mother rested her head against Teresa's shoulder while they watched the movies, the way he could tell they were touching each other under the blanket they pulled over themselves, holding hands if not worse, the blanket never long enough to cover Teresa's big feet. Those feet were bulbous and pale and always right there on the coffee table. But it was also nice to have something to watch together. He liked Hitchcock most, while Teresa was more into Bogey and Bacall, but there was some overlap. They watched movies once a week at least.

Once, he caught her looking out at the enclosures from the back porch. She held a cup of coffee and her eyes were following the pack, which was roaming, as if they had to prepare for the winter. She didn't say anything, and he didn't confront her, but he could tell in that moment that she was sensing their beauty and power. Majesty, maybe. Maybe, he thought, she wasn't so bad. Maybe he didn't hate her. Women had come in and out of his mother's life before. They lasted weeks, sometimes. Rarely months. They treated him like a nuisance or like he wasn't there at all. One of them treated him like he was a potential predator, like the worst kind of man in the making. She made snide comments and cut eyes at him. When he was just a kid. Another one, the worst, treated him like she loved him.

When he was little he would draw a lot and write stories that featured the wolves as characters. And other stories featuring sharks and whales. Underwater scenes. He could keep himself occupied for hours. He lived mostly in his own head. As a teenager he started to step out of that head a little, but it was scary outside and sometimes he would tunnel back in, now with the help of books and music. He read constantly and wrote poetry and stories sometimes, but he wasn't convinced any of them were any good. They were short and strange and not real, but they somehow felt real, like pieces of his dreams come alive. He didn't show them to anyone, but his friends still started to think of him as The Writer.

When his mother and Teresa would leave him alone in the house to go on dates or short trips, he'd sometimes have friends over while sometimes he would remain alone. When his friends came over they always wanted to see the wolves. They didn't harass them, but they didn't understand them either. He liked being alone better. He would go out and walk along the chain link fence. Sika would come to his side. He would reach down and feel her thickening fur. Once in a while he would go inside the enclosure and spend time with them. He would sit there and they would come to him, sniff him, roll around at his side. He was not afraid of them. He knew they were wild, but so was he. Sometimes, lately, he liked to get high and go into the enclosure with them. Once, he ate shrooms and went in. They moved around him, colors trailing from their backs, and he felt them with his fingertips. It was a moment of harmony, one that lasted a few hours. Afterwards he played his acoustic guitar in his dark room for hours, and he had never played so well in his life. It was fleeting, but that was why it was good.

In November it snowed, and during the last tour of the season he saw a girl he recognized from high school sitting on the observation deck watching him. She wore a puffy black jacket and a hat pulled down close to her eyes, but he still recognized her. Jennie Lee. Her family stood behind her. He felt strangely not nervous but like he should have been. He must have passed her hundreds of times at school but never paid any attention to her. They had been in the same U.S. History class together. Neither of them ever spoke during discussions. When the tour was over she came over to him and said hi. Determined not to waste this opportunity, he asked her if she would go out with him. She looked back at her family, a man, a woman, three children all younger than her, hesitated. "Ok," she said.

Families were strange. They seemed happy together. He couldn't imagine. He felt unsteady. He should have been happy, and he supposed he was, but that happiness was different than the happiness he'd expected. It was a happiness cut with fear.

On the day of their date he drove them to Friendly's near the mall. It was nice. He found himself talking for most of the time, telling her about musicians and writers he loved, writers who'd influenced how he saw the world. He told her he was writing stories and poems and she smiled, told him she would love to read them. She told him about her family, her father, who worked in the weapons industry, her mother, who was a veterinarian. She told him she didn't know what she wanted to do with her life, but he could tell that she had an idea, an idea she wouldn't tell him yet. He knew he had to crack her open and it would come out eventually. He imagined coins inside her head tumbling out into his hands.

After Friendly's he drove to the coast and they walked around and across the cold rocks. The early snow had melted but winter was in the air. The sky was purling gray. They held hands for about thirty seconds, and he felt every one of those seconds inside him. When he dropped her off he wanted to kiss her but she leaned over quick and hugged him instead.

He felt the sense memory of her hand inside his for days afterwards. He thought about her skin against his. He couldn't concentrate in class. Was this it, he wondered? Was she the one he'd been waiting for? He sat and watched *Roman Holiday* with a new appreciation. He felt like he was becoming a new person. He was late to the game of love, but now he was deep in it. He held off on masturbating, thinking of it as something childish, but he couldn't hold off for long. He imagined Teresa because that was better than imagining Jennie Lee. More respectful, somehow.

He dropped acid and did mushrooms with his friends, while staying straight and sober with Jennie Lee. He couldn't seem to move past first base with her. He couldn't bring his face close enough to hers to kiss her. He felt more shy the closer to her face he got with his face. But they held hands and they hugged, and at first that was more than enough.

On Thanksgiving she came over to his house first, in the early afternoon. They took pictures and ate turkey and stuffing. Teresa had the football game on. He saw Jennie and Teresa standing side by side, talking, and they looked not just like two different people of two different ages, but like two entirely differently species. Teresa looked like an alien come down from on high, seven feet tall at least, and Jennie looked like a normal adolescent human. It felt like worlds colliding.

After eating they went outside to feed the wolves.

"Your mom seems nice. So does Teresa," she said.

"Yeah, they're okay. Do you want to go into the enclosure with them?"

"The wolves?"

"Yeah."

She looked skeptical, but shrugged. "I guess."

He imagined writing a story about what he was doing right now, bringing this young woman he was in love with (he thought) into an enclosure with wolves. In the story the wolves would tear the girl to pieces and strew her here and there, but then he knew he wouldn't write that story, wouldn't contribute to the villainization of wolves. He knew them for what they were: animals of community and hierarchy. That hierarchy wasn't always easy. Sika had taken clear prominence in the pack, leaving the two males who'd been fighting for alpha status diminished. He opened the enclosure gate, and they walked around, then they found a place to sit where he knew his mother would not be able to see them. The half-breeds barked from their enclosure, but the wolves seemed simply curious. Jennie Lee ran her fingers through their fur, but not the way other girls her age might have, not as if they were pets. She had respect for their wild natures.

Before they left to go to her family's for their Thanksgiving, he showed Jennie his room. He'd cleaned up and taken down some of the posters, the ones that seemed childish. His acoustic stood on the guitar stand. His bed was neatly made. He turned on some music, a Nick Drake CD, and for the first time they kissed. It was not magical. At first it was nothing but awkward, all skin and spit, but he stuck with it, and after a few minutes it morphed into something more. They sat for a while on the edge of his bed smiling and holding hands. He had a brief flash of them in the future, married, with kids, but it scared him so badly he led her back outside.

Her family was kind to him, and later he kissed her goodnight.

He wished, hard, that everything could stay exactly the way it was then for as long as it possibly could, him with a brand new girlfriend, his mother happy with a woman who seemed to love her, the movie nights, the tours, Wolf Haven making enough money that his mother didn't need a second job, his father not even an afterthought, his future something out there he didn't need to think too hard about yet, but of course nothing stayed still. He tried to hold onto it even as it was already shifting and changing.

He noticed something different one morning when he woke up to go to school and found Teresa sitting at the dining room table wearing her robe. She wore loose white pants beneath the robe that almost covered her ugly feet. She'd been crying, her face uglier than he'd ever seen it. Her hands were big and he could see the veins in them. For the first time she looked like she was closer to his mother's age, not his. She looked like a full-blown adult. In fact, she looked kind of old. He thought for a second that his mother had made her that way, that she was aging this woman, but he knew that couldn't be true.

Then he came home to them shouting at each other. They slammed the door of their bedroom, but he could still hear them behind the door. He'd never heard his mother shout before, and it frightened him. She was a whole different woman. She'd had a few arguments with her other women, but not like this. This was new. She had never yelled at him the way she was yelling at Teresa, her voice on the verge of cracking. Things were thrown. Something shattered.

He walked outside to spend time with the wolves.

He realized that, in a way, in some kind of way at least, he loved Teresa. She was nothing but his mother's girlfriend, and they'd hardly even had a one-on-one conversation together, but she'd become part of his life. She had nestled in like a tick into the skin of one of the wolves. She had become part of his life, and now he knew she was going to be leaving.

First there were weeks of fighting. They were always at each other. They tried to watch one movie, *Vertigo*, but halfway through they went into their bedroom and yelled at each other. She had cheated on his mother. There was another woman involved. She hadn't meant to, it hadn't meant anything, couldn't they just forget it? He almost felt sorry for her. He was in love with Jennie Lee, who was moving away with her family in two months. For her father's job.

Everything had suddenly become tragic.

When Teresa finally left, she went out back with bolt cutters, and she cut open the gates of the enclosures, first of the wolves and then of the halfbreeds. They were able to reclose the wolves' enclosure before anyone escaped—the animals were accustomed to their territory, didn't expect any more in their lifetimes, but the halfbreeds fled immediately into the woods.

The next summer, Jennie Lee no more than a memory, Teresa gone from their lives, sometimes he saw them in the distance, a flash of muzzle, a flank moving fast through the shadows. Sometimes he heard them barking, snarling, fighting. They marauded. He realized that he loved them, too. He'd never named them, but he had loved them.

Beasts

She would not know that Coyote was a fixture of Native American folklore until college, when she would read about the trickster with a mixture of interest and suppressed horror. Her mother told her coyote stories as she lay in her childhood bed in the gray house on Route 9, stories set to the rhythm of headlights flashing across the ceiling throughout the night. In her mother's stories the coyote was not a trickster but simple evil, ranging across the New Jersey pinelands with bloodied muzzle, hungry for children who wandered away from their homes. Her mother smoked cigarettes and drank scotch, but those two smells could not cover the heady, animal scent of her mother's body.

They had five dogs that lived inside a section of the yard enclosed by a chain-link fence. In Nell's memory, she saw them clustered together in a ball, a bundle of legs and tails and teeth, none named. They were all old and feeble, and she worried that someone would leave the gate open, that the coyote would get them.

The coyote came down from the north, her mother said in a sandpaper voice. The coyote traveled at night, always alone. He was a rangy bastard with big paws, his muzzle bright red with fresh blood. He had been eating children for so long he didn't know that eating children was wrong. The children's bodies gave him strength, their little bones snapping in his jaws, their skulls crunching. He could slip between tree trunks like water, fast and silent. His hair was silver and shone in the moonlight, but people saw him only if he wanted them to see him.

To Nell, in her bed, the coyote seemed both frightening and pitiable. He was so alone. After her mother left her for the night, Nell would listen for him out the window, picking his way through the darkness. Woods separated their backyard from the parkway—thin pine trees grew thick, covered with ivy that lost its leaves in the winter and clung to tree trunks like pale snakes, sometimes thicker than the tree trunks themselves.

In the afternoon, Nell would get off the elementary school bus and sit on the back steps looking into the woods. If she looked long enough, eyes would appear from between the interstices of branches. Winters seemed to take up half the year—long months, gray skies. It rarely snowed in South Jersey, but the earth would give everything up. She watched television, hoping it would drown out the world behind her, waiting for her mother to return from work.

Once, while her mother was driving home from the food store, they saw a coyote dart across the road, a sleek, rangy animal with a silver mane, similar to but very different from their dogs. See, her mother said. I told you he was out there. The coyote ran beneath the powerlines, fast. She saw him, then he was gone.

Looking back on it, her childhood appeared shrouded. Her past took on the tone of a fairytale: wordless menace.

When Nell had her own daughter, she told Reina stories that mixed the coyote of her mother's stories with Coyote of Native American folklore. The California foothills was a world away from South Jersey, but they were neither more nor less wild. Her daughter's eyes widened with wonder. The coyote watches whatever we do, she heard herself saying, and he laughs a lot. Most of what we do is foolish. The coyote feasts alone in the woods. He comes to us because he has to come to us. Because we want him.

She was not guilty that she was telling lies about her past, because the past was not settled. Maybe she was what she claimed to be—indigenous. After earning her PhD, she secured a tenure track position teaching indigenous literature at a small college in Michigan, and her family followed her. In the mirror her shapeless reflection flickered, sometimes catching for a moment on an image of teeth and muzzle. Flesh dissolved into story. Her students either loved or hated her.

Reina was encouraged to walk the wild woods of the Upper Peninsula alone. They could not have stopped her if they wanted to. Her black hair grew out past her eyes. She learned to track animals, to read their traces in the earth. The earth retained the memory of beasts. Some day, Reina would tell her own stories, would discover a new wild world to bring back with her, but for now they pulled apart a little. Mother and daughter. A dance. Shadowboxing.

When Nell's mother died, she and Reina sat on a train, traveling toward a new sense of mortality. Nothing ever really ends, Nell told her daughter. Circles. Cycles of energy. You can hold the unknown away from you, but that has no real impact on danger. Reina murmured in her sleep. She would marry a bear and slit the bear open and live inside him through the long cold winter. The sky would glaze over and turn gray while hundreds of geese flew above them. The earth didn't forget anything. Nell held her daughter in her arms and listened to her murmured words. What else was there?

Our Lady of Eternal Sorrows

On the Saturday morning after Tanya Koval went missing, the fathers formed search parties and spread throughout the neighborhood, dividing it into quadrants. They checked inside sheds and the corners of yards, hunting for a flash of red. She had last been seen walking home from school wearing a red sateen jacket. They all hoped to find the body. None of them believed she was still alive. It was an era of danger, realized. Their hearts beat hard, ready to stop at the sight of her, to call out, to turn her over and look at her face, notice the marks on her neck from a strangling, her jeans pulled down past pale thighs.

They picked through their neighbors' backyards, secretly thrilled to cross property lines, stepping over stone walls and the invisible lines of propriety, peeking into neighbors' sheds, taking note of the markers of status within. The Aucoins owned a riding mower, John Deere no less, whereas the Morriseys had a rusty set of lawn darts and old plastic bags of moldering leaves in their shed. The smell of gasoline and rotting plywood in shadows.

Bill Harte found a dead possum in back of the Williamsons', near a little creek, its mouth open, its tiny teeth, white and pearlescent, frightening. Gary Rounder found a live snake, black and moist, slithering through a patch of half disintegrated leaves. He told no one. Gary felt guilty even though he hadn't done anything, had certainly not killed the girl, though he'd seen her around and had imagined things. All the fathers had.

THOSE OF US OLD ENOUGH to join the search made a bee-line for the pits, an open span of turned up land left over from the construction of the neighborhood. Tanya's older brother, Chris, a senior who'd been accepted at the University of New Hampshire on a wrestling scholarship, worked his way through the woods beyond the pits, bushwhacking, branches whipping back behind him. If he bushwhacked far enough he'd reach the Sprung River, where a rope swing hung from the limb of an old maple tree, even though the river ran only three feet at its deepest. Every summer one of us broke an arm trying to jump in. The rest of us searched the pits, remembering when we'd ridden our bikes out here as kids. We didn't usually see the pits in the daylight anymore. We were grouchy and wanted to return to bed, but we also wanted to be the one to find her, wanted to be able to tell that story.

But it was Chris who found her. First he found the red jacket, placed atop brambles like a beacon, sleeves outstretched so it looked as if a torso was still inside. The sateen was spotless, the red of a fresh holly berry or a cardinal. Her jeans and panties had been balled up in the mud under the brambles. And Tanya herself, or Tanya's body, was curled on her side, naked, her hair, usually so carefully kept, gone wild, covering half her face. The hair was the only thing alive about her; it wanted to hide the rest of her. He saw a jaw, a cheek, but not her eyes. It had rained the night before, and her bare body was muddy.

"What the *fuck*?" he said, the words falling from his mouth. "Over here!" he yelled.

Fathers barreled through the underbrush. Within a minute men were surrounding Chris, pushing him, gently but firmly, away. Mrs. Garrison led him out of the copse, her arm around his shoulders, while Mrs. Marsh hurried over with a pink blanket they wrapped Tanya's body inside, hiding her face.

Later, some of us would claim we'd seen the body, that we had seen her legs ripped open, her pussy gashed, her tits cut off, but the adults formed a protective barrier around the body, as if it were a totem that could teach us more about the world than we were ready to know. No one younger than Chris Koval saw her body. It was wrapped in the pink blanket, carried out by a phalanx of adults, slid into the back of the Gere's paneled station wagon, and driven straight to the St. Anselm's Police Department, Mr. Gere at the wheel feeling sanctified by his important position in the tragedy.

POLICE ARRIVED WITHIN TEN MINUTES of the body being found to search the crime scene, starting at the entrance to the pits, at the end of the Victorian Street cul-de-sac. They cordoned off the brambles where the body had been found, the little patch of fieldgrass below a copse of evergreens. They collected the wadded jeans and panties, the sateen jacket, the bra and shirt found in a ball ten feet away, in separate evidence bags to be tested for fingerprints, blood typing, and the earliest forms of DNA testing. They were frustrated that the body had been moved before they could inspect it. The crime scene had been compromised, first by the removal of the body then by the obliterating footsteps of dozens of people, so their chances of finding the killer were already seriously diminished. Why were people so *stupid*, they wondered, putting their hands on their hips, shaking their heads, regarding the crime scene. It was almost like they didn't want the killer to be caught.

We watched the police with a new suspicion born of nothing in particular. Just a feeling. We were God-fearing, rule-following people (mostly) who had always looked upon law enforcement as our protectors, but we doubted they could do anything in this case. They hadn't prevented the atrocity from happening, so why should they be expected to solve it?

DURING MASS AT OUR LADY OF ETERNAL SORROWS that Sunday, Father Proster made references to a local tragedy. His homily was on the virtues of community, and, even though he didn't name the crime or the victim, we all knew what and who he was referring to. As he spoke, Proster's glance fell often on the empty space in the pew where the Kovals customarily sat.

In the following weeks, Our Lady of Eternal Sorrows would pray for Tanya Koval following every Mass, and she would become the tacit or overt focus of many of Father Proster's homilies. Proster remembered the girl. He'd watched her while giving homilies, or when he was performing some other part of the service, the Liturgy of the Eucharist or the Liturgy of the Word, and had wondered how his voice was reverberating in her ribcage, what effect he was having on her. She had been a distinctive-looking young woman, with the iciest blue eyes he'd ever seen. Those eyes had stared up at him from out of the pew for years. He remembered her as a child, her eyes always more adult than the rest of her. Who knows what was happening behind them? Something, surely, not entirely holy.

Following Mass every Sunday, Father Proster would shake hands with our families on the steps leading to the parking lot, in front of the large, modern church with its angles of tinted glass and planes of brown wood. Proster was kind and patient, warm and friendly; sometimes he would be out on the steps for an hour or more. After the last family had drifted away, back to our station wagons and sedans, he would return to his office and crawl out of his vestments. He would sit in a comfortable shirt and pants in his office in the rear of the church, looking out the window, contemplating.

WE WERE HELD IN SUSPENSION, a collective state of shock, following the discovery of Tanya Koval's body. After church on the Sunday following the discovery, children walked dogs, rode bikes, played capture the flag. Families did yardwork, picking up deadfall from trees, preparing flowerbeds, raking out dead leaves from the understory. Some of us burned branches and leaves in metal drums, others raked them into piles we hauled into our backyards, miniature wildernesses full of ferns and stone walls, some featuring creeks, some backed up to the real wilderness.

A pick-up game of tackle football started in the side yard of the Hendersons, the kindly old couple who gave out apples on Halloween, and a game of street hockey broke out on Georgian Avenue. We all stopped whenever we heard a car, looking up, freezing. Sometimes we didn't need to hear anything in order to freeze; shadows passed over us and we stopped as one, looking around, embarrassed. Tackles were not as vicious as usual. Trash talk was milder. People walking past each other on the street smiled sadly, shook their heads, and sometimes exchanged greetings, but suspicion had grown up between us, snaking like weeds through all our thoughts.

EVERY MOTHER PREPARED SOMETHING to bring to the Kovals. Tuna casseroles, potatoes au gratin, lima bean casserole. Various pies and brownies. Chilis and soups and bread. Banana bread, cranberry nut bread, orange walnut bread. They made things from recipes cut out of *Family Circle* and *Woman's Day* and delivered the food in casserole dishes under foil or in foil bread pans that did not need to be returned. Chris answered the door and took the food from the mothers' hands, thanking them politely before closing the door again. He was such a good boy, athletic and intelligent and so good looking. He was clearly broken up by the death of his sister. The mothers could see the memory of finding his sister's body on his face, where it would sit for the rest of his life, turning him ugly as he aged. Secretly they were thrilled by it. They refused to acknowledge those feelings, though they came out in various ways, in bedrooms and living rooms for the next couple weeks.

The mothers imagined the Kovals, Peter and Shelly, inside the house, in the addition they'd had built, an airy, open space featuring a large-screen television and overstuffed furniture, with Pergo floors. It was where Tanya, after pushing the furniture to the edges of the room, had practiced her dancing. The mothers imagined the Kovals sitting on the overstuffed furniture staring into space. Or they pictured Mr. Koval alone in the basement in his workroom, pretending to work on something but really just sitting staring at an old picture album, the pages sticking together as he tried to turn them. Pictures of his sweet little girl throughout the years. Her first dance outfit. Sleeping in a onesie in her crib. Looking up with a toothless grin from a yellow-tiled bathtub (before they'd had the bathroom remodeled). There were pictures of her with friends, during Christmas parties, wearing Halloween costumes (a ballerina one year, a pirate the next), in the mountains when they would go camping.

The mothers imagined Mrs. Koval in the darkened bedroom sobbing, or unable to sob. Paralyzed, not even there. Not a person, not a woman, anymore. Fallen into a dark space between one part of her life and another, one she could not begin to imagine, a life as the mother of a dead girl. The mothers imagined her ashen face, her empty eyes. The unending pain of a mother. The failure and shame that would form a bubble around her for the rest of her life.

They imagined the open door to the girl's bedroom, her things scattered around, and thought of their own daughters' messy bedrooms. The heaped clothes of a teenage girl, and such a pretty one, too, her leggings from dance class, her leotards, designer jeans, shirts and bras and panties in brightly colored heaps here and there, messy but not messy

messy, not the way boys' rooms got. There would be no food left on the floors, though maybe there would be a glass of Kool-Aid on the dresser. There would be posters on the walls, pop stars, maybe Sean Cassidy, a memento from her youth, maybe the poster for a ballet she dreamed of performing in one day, a brightly colored plastic radio on the dresser next to a matching Princess phone, her cans of Aqua Net and bottles of body spray, a mirror edged with photographs, some strips of three from photobooths at Hampton Beach. A Polaroid of her dressed like Madonna in a half shirt last Halloween, with three friends, her little tan stomach peeking through black lace.

Hidden in various places around her room would be half-finished packs of cigarettes and liquor bottles, maybe marijuana, a small baggie of brown weed shoved into her old turtle-shaped retainer case. A handful of Valium she'd stolen from her friend's mother's medicine cabinet, expired but still effective. The names of boys would be scrawled inside her notebooks. Her first name linked to boys' last names. Tanya Stalling and Tanya Thibodault and Tanya Moore. Some of the names had the ring of porn stars. Maybe there were more sinister things hidden in more secret places. Letters exchanged between her and a stranger, a shadowy man who wrote like a lover but looked like a monster.

The mothers wanted there to be some explanation for the incident, some way they could pin at least some of the blame on her. They hoped there were no dark secrets like that, for the mother's sake, but they hoped so, for their own. They wanted the girl to be complicit, in order to put their own girls' innocence in contrast. They wanted to believe, despite all the evidence of their own experience and the copious evidence of human history, in the inviolability of good daughters.

ON SUNDAY NIGHT WE SLIPPED out of our houses, edging out back doors or climbing through windows. If our parents were negligent or if we were old enough, on the verge of adulthood, we stepped out the front door and walked down the middle of the street. We lit cigarettes and feathered our hair with combs kept in the back pockets of our jeans. We wore denim or leather jackets. We stepped over or ducked under the yellow caution tape stretched across the entrance to the pits, or we walked around the entrance and slipped between the trees on either side. The tape was an attractant, not a deterrent. Bottles clanked inside bookbags, baggies of weed were wedged in the front pockets of acid-washed jeans. It was too cold for partying outdoors, and we wouldn't have done it if not for the discovery of the body, but now there was no question: we rubbed our hands together and braved the chill wind. This was an obligation, a solemn rite. There was no planning. No one had to be told to gather; we simply gathered.

We hoped Chris Koval would show up, that he would come down to the pits and tell us the story of finding his sister's body. We imagined him walking through the pits, lifting up the branches, seeing the bright red jacket on the bush in front of him, imagined how it must have felt. Like something blooming in his chest, a wild weed sprouting from his lungs. An overwhelming physical sensation, like being on the edge of a cliff, or beside a waterfall. The way his breath must have stopped, the way his brain must have struggled to make sense of the body laid out before him. We hoped he would come and perform the suffering victim for us, though we suspected he wouldn't. We wouldn't, if we were him. We would hole away inside ourselves and maybe never come out again.

We built a bonfire at the edge of the pits, fifteen feet from where the body had been discovered, arranging chunks of deadwood into a pyre. Our faces looked normal at first, until the fire flapped in the wind and changed our expressions, shadows twisting mouths from grins into grimaces and back again. We made pilgrimages to the spot where the body had been found, as if it were sacred, kneeling to touch still-matted grass. We could see her shape in the grass. We wanted to fit our own bodies inside the shape, and we would have if we were alone, but that seemed disrespectful, and we were here to pay homage. She had died for us.

We told stories about Tanya Koval, most apocryphal. In the stories, she was either a saint or a slut, often both at the same time. She had slept with multiple boys at once or she was a virgin, more pure than any girl could ever hope to be. Holding out for love, if not marriage. She was the most talented dancer any of us had ever known—there was consensus on that. She had practiced for hours every week. She talked about someday dancing professionally, and it didn't seem like a pipedream, the way so many of our dreams seemed. She had auditioned for dance companies in Boston and New York City and was waiting to hear back. Some of the girls in her dance class had been jealous of her, had hated how easy she made everything seem, how perfect her body had been for everything she wanted it to do, but now they talked about how supportive they had been, and how kind Tanya had been, not stuck-up at all, even though she was obviously so much better than they were. They talked about how they had all lifted her up and wanted her to do great things, supported her ambitions. They had been proud of her.

Not only was Tanya a talented dancer, she was also a brilliant student, with a 4.0 GPA, taking honors classes, Latin, even, who had earned a perfect score on the verbal section of the PSAT and a nearly perfect score on the math. She was going to go to Harvard or someplace like that. An Ivy, for sure. She had planned to see the world and help poor people in other countries, and she would have done it, too. It wasn't just talk with Tanya, the way it was with some of us. She had truly cared about poverty and the fate of the world. She had loved everyone. She had clearly been the best of us. So why *her*?

The girls imagined themselves as Tanya, while the boys imagined raping and killing her, in more or less detail. We couldn't stop ourselves. The fire bounced off our eyes. There were smirks that passed quickly, hidden in the mutating expressions caused by the fire. Some of the girls broke down and had to be comforted.

We couldn't believe that this had happened *here*, but secretly we had all hoped for something like it, had, in fact, been waiting all our lives for it. We'd grown up on stories of abduction. Psychotic hitchhikers and serial killers. There had been a grisly murder on Ferndale Avenue five years earlier, in a neighborhood not far away, and we would sit in the backseats of our parents' cars watching the street sign pass and imagine things, scared, intrigued, made aware of the darkness of the world all around us: easy to forget when all we saw were identical houses and bucolic nature. We wondered if this murder was connected to that, earlier one. Another raped and murdered girl. Had the Ferndale killer ever been caught, we wondered?

Growing up we would talk redrum and chant Bloody Mary in mirrors three times at midnight. Some of us had older brothers who snuck us into *Halloween* and *Friday the 13th*. Some of us read Stephen King novels about vampires, rabid dogs, and haunted cemeteries, or we passed around Satanic Bibles. Satanic rites were supposedly being performed in the woods, in the northern part of St. Anselm's, near the pond. We had expected tragedy to touch our lives at some point—the only thing we hadn't known was who the victim would be. We had all secretly dreaded and hoped that we were marked.

Some of us paired off and found dark places in the woods to fuck, holding on to the rough bark of trees, our bodies on the edge of control. Many of us got so drunk we puked. We played music on the boombox someone had brought out to the pits, mostly heavy metal, Mötley Crüe and Dio because that's how we felt. Past midnight we mellowed into Led Zeppelin, acoustic songs interspersed with louder electric blues. We couldn't believe how good and full and alive we felt. The world had taken on an edge we'd never felt before. We felt special, chosen, and we were relieved that chosen didn't mean dead.

WHEN WE RETURNED TO SCHOOL on Monday, we felt marked by our proximity to tragedy. None of us, aside from Chris Koval, had seen the body, but we all felt as if we had. We were all prone to false memories. Her pale, naked body, violated, contorted, almost unrecognizable. We saw her dead eyes wide open in her dead face, icy blank blue stares.

Some of us took the experience as a badge of honor and told anyone who would listen what we had (supposedly) seen. Clots of curious students formed in the hallways of the elementary, jr. high, and high schools. We talked about the body with a kind of brazen care, tenders of a strange and bloody legacy. Our listeners shook their heads slowly, mouths falling open, or their faces hardened as they tried not to let the images enter and affect them. The images spread virally, all of us picturing poor, dead Tanya Koval's body, the parts of her body that had just developed mangled and mutilated. Some of us pictured her violently, others in loving and precise detail.

At least half of us realized we had been in love with Tanya Koval, even though she had never been on a date because boys feared her. She was so sure of herself, so smart, so beautiful. We balked at the word, but it was the only one that fit: Tanya was not cute or pretty; she possessed the fully realized beauty of a grown woman. The girls who desired her kept that desire to themselves—it was not an age of Gay-Straight Alliances and LGBT Pride. It was an era of deep closeting and deeper shame, the first rumblings of the AIDS epidemic at the periphery of our lives about to sweep across the country.

Others of us felt marked in a different way, as if we were responsible for the murder, or were potential next victims. We did not talk, to anyone about anything. We skulked down hallways like sharks, silent, hovering, never stopping, aware of the shadows that stretched behind us even under the fluorescent lights of the school. We kept our knowledge shut tightly inside our heads, and, while we hated those who commanded a crowd, we also recognized the impulse for attention, for the sharing of shadows. Hatred, wonder, and confusion mixed inside us. Lust and sorrow and fear.

It suddenly seemed as if the world was and always had been dangerous; we just hadn't realized until now. We looked at our teachers in a new way. We became skeptical of men. Mr. O'Dwyer could probably rape and kill any one of us, and he probably wanted to. He probably spent half the time he was supposed to be teaching planning it. Mr. Sanders would probably drown us, holding our heads under the water with his large, sure hand until we stopped struggling. Mr. Roberts, the Industrial Arts teacher, could use his tools to hack us limb from limb before he disposed of our bodies. We pictured him like a mad butcher, hands and work apron cloaked in blood.

We had entered a world full of obscure desires. We were not sure, yet, whether we would ever escape that world. Maybe, we thought, this *was* the world.

IT WAS IMPOSSIBLE NOT TO WONDER what the mortician had to do in order to make her face presentable, something like what it had looked like alive. We wondered what had been done to the body. The mortician wouldn't have to make the body whole again, because it was covered with a pink dress, hands overlapping on her stomach, lace details on the long sleeves and around the torso. The dress was sweet and strange. Strange, because it wasn't a dress Tanya Koval would have worn in real life. No girl her age that year would have. The dress was frilly and girly, and the pink did not complement the skin that had somehow retained a tan throughout the winter.

No doubt the dress had been selected by Mrs. Koval, who stood beside the open casket, blank-faced, her soul having slipped out of her body and run through the floorboards. The girls noticed how pretty Mrs. Koval was—or had been at one time. At one time she would have attracted the attention of all the men in any room she walked into. The girls didn't know anything about her, but imagined a romantic past for her. International travel, a series of love affairs ending with Mr. Koval. And Mr. Koval… they'd never noticed him before, either. A middle manager at Digital, he was actually kind of handsome. He didn't have the beer belly so many fathers had, he still had all of his hair, salt and pepper and feathered the same way his son's was, and he looked strong and stoic, a man who held everything inside him.

A sense of wonder pervaded the room, the biggest room of Andretti's Funeral Home. The carpet was thin and green, floral details around the edges. The chairs were wingback, upholstered green. There were "Italian" flourishes, columns built into each corner of the room, landscape paintings of cliffside Mediterranean villages on the walls. There were too many flowers in the room, bunches and bundles, bouquets, the odors cloying. Everyone in town, it seemed, had sent flowers. Sending flowers was an easy way to appear to care about the tragic death of one of their children.

We were protective of Tanya, dismissive of anyone who came from other parts of town, even if they had some claim on her: the girls in her dance class, old friends from her Girl Scout troop or softball team. We formed protective circles around the basket full of photographs, around the guest book, around the body in the casket. People from outside the neighborhood paid their respects and left quickly, sensing they were not welcome here.

The girls remembered times they hung out with Tanya, when she'd been one of four or five girls prowling the mall, wandering through the amusement park, or massing at Friendly's, sitting in booths eating sundaes and laughing. They remembered how she always got the most attention, how jealous they'd been of her. Spiteful, envious, petty. She had not brought out the best in them. They thought about how cool she'd been, how she hadn't cared when boys looked at her and flirted, how cold she could be to them. The way she treated boys was funny and awe-inspiring. She had power over them but refused to use it. Sometimes, they knew, she spent time with older boys who had already graduated. Doing what, they wondered. They wondered about the secret life they were sure she had. (Part of it *had* to be her fault, right?) Their favorite times were when they would drink wine coolers in the woods or someone's basement when someone's parents were away, and they would tell jokes and stories and laugh. They laughed so much. She had been so much *fun*.

Stories were told at the funeral home, too, and, like the stories told around the bonfire, these stories were mostly lies. Sweet lies, but lies all the same. How kind and perceptive and funny Tanya Koval had been. How perfect in every way. Her unbounded potential. Her particular beauty. Her dance teacher, Mrs. Anna, broke down in front of everyone and had to be led away by her husband, a burly man underdressed in a gray polo shirt and black slacks. We all noticed the bulge of a gun in his pocket and wondered.

WE EXPECTED ANOTHER ONE OF US to be plucked, at any moment. Murders rarely came singly during that time period. Murders came in matched sets, or in large collections. All murders were potentially serial. We imagined sisters or friends abducted. The girls were obviously in the most danger, but the boys were not safe either. There was no guarantee that the killer was after only girls, although, knowing what we knew, that seemed most likely. Girls were always in the most danger. That was the world we'd been born into: a girl-hating, girl-abducting, girl-devouring world.

Now the girls' bodies were even more endangered than usual. They were being looked at, weighed, judged as meat and as potential vessels of pain and hatred every second of every day, even alone. They'd all heard what had been done to Tanya Koval, in detail. Some of the stories were true, while others were extreme versions of the truth, a truth brought into being by dark desire. Two things were perfectly clear: Tanya Koval had been a virgin, and she had been raped after she was murdered, which made it all even more horrible.

Some girls started wearing baggy clothes, sweatpants and their boyfriends' jeans, while others dressed the way they always had, the way they were "supposed" to. They did their hair up with Aqua Net, elaborate routines that ate hours out of every week, and wore clothes bought at Merry Go Round, Benetton, and Banana Republic. Sweaters and stirrup pants. They descended on the local mall in small groups, laughing, sharing Orange Juliuses and talking about boys, the way they always had. Pretending things were normal was a defense mechanism. What else were they supposed to do? Freak out all the time?

Some of them dreamed of escaping, of going to college and "becoming" something… but what? They didn't want to be what their mothers were: housewives, nurses, or teachers, or working alongside men at the cutting edge of whatever industry they entered, battling for respect. The first female engineer or the first female doctor or the first female whatever. They wanted unlimited options they knew they would never get. They pretended things were the same as they had always been. And in a way they were right. The murder of

Tanya Koval simply threw reality into a starker light. Their limited lives were always already endangered.

AT THE LOCAL CEMETERY, schoolkids did tracings on vellum in full sun, wearing windbreakers, hooded sweatshirts, and jeans, their hair tousled by the wind. They traced obsolete names—Captain Clifford Crowninshield, Elizabeth Powter, Eliza This and Ebenezer That and Celia Something Else, dead babies, dead mothers, dead fathers, 9yrs, 84yrs—and skulls with wings sprouting from their earholes. The oldest headstones dated from the 1700s, the time of St. Anselm's founding. The schoolkids watched the small funeral caravan pass. The burial was restricted to immediate family.

The children stopped now and then to glance over at the people clustered around the open grave. Only those of us from the neighborhood knew who was being buried, her name already legend: Tanya Koval, The Dead Girl. The others thought about members of their own families who'd died. They watched the group walk back to their cars and drive away, the little caravan exiting the cemetery again.

The morbid among us wanted to walk over to the coffin and open it, wanted to look at The Dead Girl inside, to gaze upon death. We imagined The Dead Girl would haunt the cemetery, wearing the frilly pink dress she'd been stuffed in (we'd heard stories from older siblings) forever. She'd been murdered, and worse, whatever that meant. We imagined coming back to the cemetery when it was dark and getting spooked out, the girl a skull with wings that nipped at our ankles and dive-bombed our heads.

We were disappointed when our teachers herded us back toward the school buses, robbing us of seeing the coffin lowered into the ground and the undertakers spilling in the first shovelfuls of dirt. We imagined the sound of dirt hitting the coffin lid, the reverberating thud while pebbles scattered to the side. We imagined the girl inside, dead Tanya

Koval, opening her eyes, looking up and all around her at the darkness, and screaming.

AT EASTER, WE THOUGHT ABOUT JESUS rising from the dead. The story behind the holiday seemed more real now. We imagined the flesh and meat of the story more clearly, the way He would arise, His side coated with tacky blood scabbing over the wound, the pains in His joints, His ribcage aching with each labored breath, the blood in His matted hair, the feeling of filth covering His body like microscopic bugs. How thirsty He must have been. We imagined Tanya Koval rising from the dead in a similar manner, the door to her coffin flung open and Tanya stepping out with her dancer's legs, in her pink dress, hair dusted with grave-dirt. Maybe Tanya Koval was the Jesus we needed in the late twentieth century. Maybe she could take our new, modern sins. Maybe she was our sacrifice.

We had built a shrine in the woods where her body had been found. There were several teddy bears holding hearts, some stuffed bunnies that got matted and muddy following the first rain, two pairs of old, pink ballet slippers: small, wrinkled, fetal shapes. There were also darker tokens of a more dangerous past. Packs of Marlboro Lights. Small airplane bottles of Southern Comfort. Someone had carved "I fucked Tanya Koval" into one of the nearby trees. It must have taken hours, each letter cut down to heartwood. Sap seeped from the letters. The dedication was impressive, though no one believed it. Tanya had been a virgin when she was raped. Someone else had left a long note professing her love. "You never knew, and now you never will," the note ended. The paper was pink, perfumed, and folded, and it had been left after the first rain. Within weeks it would be pulp.

We rode dirt bikes around the makeshift track in the pits, shivering each time we passed the corner that led to the copse. There were nightly parties of varying sizes, from a couple lonely wastoids standing around a tiny fire passing a joint back and forth to a hundred kids, most from outside the neighborhood, tourists who wanted to feel the edge of the mortal world, gathered around bonfires that blazed in the night sky. It seemed strange that the birds had returned and new life was burgeoning, the buds of trees unfurling to become leaves again, while death still lurked in our midst.

WHEN THE AMUSEMENT PARK at Nocambie Lake opened for the season, half of us flocked to our summer jobs there, getting rides from parents or carpooling in old Fords and Volkswagens. Some of us had worked beside Tanya Koval the previous summer. We remembered her in the required white polo that contrasted nicely with her tanned skin, her vibrant blue eyes. Her skin had taken on a bronze cast over the summer that made her eyes even more prominent. She'd been perfect and mysterious and desirable, and most of the boys regretted that we'd never at least given it a try. No one had ever seen her with a boy, and only other very pretty girls knew how lonely she must have been.

We worked the cotton candy machine, our hands and arms becoming coated with invisible sugar until the coats crusted and cracked, or we ran the rides. Sometimes college kids who worked at the food stands and the restaurant by the lake shore would entice high school kids back to dorm rooms or into the woods to get high or fuck or both. There was always the possibility of, and sometimes the reality of, transgression.

We forgot all about Tanya Koval for days at a time. Sometimes no one (aside from the Kovals) thought about her at all. We thought about whoever had murdered her and gotten away with it, but less and less. Life was returning to normal, shadows retracting back into the woods. Groups of us drove to the White Mountains or Salisbury Beach, and we worked our summer jobs at the race track or the amusement park. We met in the pits at different times, on different nights, different configurations of people with little overlap. Groups were becoming more defined. There were now heads and jocks who wouldn't talk to each other. Music largely defined us. Hair metal and speed metal, post-punk and pop.

It amazed us that the world could go on exactly as it had before.

THEN THE MURDERER WAS CAUGHT. A local man, one of the fathers. A predator in our midst. He was Portuguese American. Like many of the fathers, he'd moved from the mill city over the state border to St. Anselm's, and he'd lived first on Fernwood Avenue. He had three sons and a wife who had never suspected anything, not really.

Reading news about Richard Piras, the murderer, the fathers felt stirrings. They would never have done what Piras had done, yet part of them felt like they had. Guilt ran inside them like molten steel being molded into strange shapes. They had watched the girl walking in the neighborhood. They had seen her among other girls and they had seen her alone. They saw the friends of their daughters wearing miniskirts or tight stirrup pants or short shorts, and they had desires. They knew it was wrong, and most of them brushed those desires aside, but reading what Piras had done… they were jealous, some of them. All of them, a little.

They turned on news radio as they drove down Routes 93 and 495 toward Chelmsford and Braintree, where they worked in plants developing new ways to kill people, and listened to stories about Richard Piras. No one would have suspected him, and if he'd been smarter, he could have gotten away with it. They'd nabbed him with DNA. His sperm inside the girl. Piras was quiet, a good man to all appearances, the Little League coach of some of their sons. And a good one, too. They had trusted him with their boys.

They thought about the woods at 3:30 in the afternoon, sunlight falling on her skin.

They hated Richard Piras and thought he was the worst kind of trash—thought he should get the death penalty, be fried in the electric chair. They hated him more because they recognized themselves in him. They sat looking at their daughters across the dinner table, closing their eyes against all the possibilities in the world. How could they protect their daughters from things that moved even inside them? They were all prone to the same virus. Popular movies were full of it. They thought of the poster for *Jaws*, the pretty girl skinny dipping in the ocean, her long limbs, her golden hair, the monster lurking in the water beneath her. They thought of the perfection of limbs, pale and skinny, that could be pulled apart. They lay awake at night while their wives slept, imagining the act, the images a carousel, their hands pressed against her mouth, yanking down her jeans, pressing themselves inside her. They jerked off, sometimes with their wives sleeping beside them, snoring peacefully, the danger of being caught ramping up the pleasure, sometimes in the bathroom or in workrooms, hearts throbbing painfully, hardly able to believe how disgusting they were, how abject. They half-hoped and half-feared they would kill themselves in this way, the veins in their temples bursting. It would be just recompense for what they made possible in the world.

On weekends, they acted as they always had, playing catch with their sons, taking their families out for ice cream, going to the movies. They sat in restaurants laughing. They sat in pews at various churches, listening to Father Proster if they were Catholic, but not really listening, thoughts wandering, eyes on the arms and bare shoulders of teenage girls, the girls' faces, their hair, feeling unholy. Before Richard Piras, they had not looked, had not contemplated, and now they blamed him. It was *his* fault. He had brought this into the world. But of course he hadn't. They had been contemplating all along.

THE MURDER AFFECTED ALL OF OUR LIVES. For most of us, the effect was tangential. We now felt the constant presence of shadows and monsters. We came to realize that we were and always had been in a labyrinth, and that the Minotaur was around any corner, ready to rape and kill us, ready to rape and kill our family and friends, ready to rape and kill our own children, if we were to have them. We thought about the lost girl at odd moments. Tanya Koval, the name a signifier of so many things. She would become our patron saint, our lady of eternal sorrows. We would pay homage to her. She would become a perfect image in our mind. What we were and what we could have been, what we should have been, what we could never be.

Whenever we called home, from college or our later adult lives, we would get news from our parents, who all remained behind. How Richard Piras, the murderer, got cancer ten years after being sent to Walpole, how he died in prison, was buried in the prison cemetery. How the Piras family moved away. Some of us returned home and buried the knowledge inside us, learned to lived with it, while others fanned out across the country, carrying the contagion with us. It could burst out in moments of spectacular violence.

It would come to seem like, and then to be, a story out of another era, the 1980s, a time of bright yellow wallpaper, brown furniture, synthetic pop. A period in which death pervaded our culture. The Vietnam War had just wound down, leaving behind veterans wounded in every conceivable way. There were intermittent race riots in cities across the country. Terrorists were hijacking airplanes and holding passengers hostage on hot tarmacs. Drugs had turned deadly: angel dust leading young men to jump out windows, crack ravaging entire city neighborhoods. One life did not mean all that much in the big scheme of things, but in our lives it did.

Cold Cold, Bright Bright

It was cold in Nova Scotia that winter, cold straight through, every day cold. Often we had to crack a skim of ice in the toilet before flushing. The pipes withstood freezing only because I had insulated them all, removing the registers from the floorboards and wrapping cozy sleeves around them. I crawled into tight spaces to wrap the pipes in the basement. Mr. Tinberg said we were lucky that I was so small, so nimble, even at my age. He looked at my hands as we were eating dinner; the way that I worked my chopsticks seemed to amaze him. "I am really impressed with your hands, Yen," he would say. "They are remarkable. There is a fluidity there." I would nod and smile. Yes sir, Mr. Tinberg. They are nice hands but so, so old. An old woman's hands. I suspected that he thought of my hands while he wrote music in his room, all day. He was so locked up, so locked in, I wondered what he could have to write about or think about, but he told me that the music was like a river running underground and he just had to tap into it—it was always there. I liked music, but, I have to admit, not his music, which often did not sound like music at all but like screeching birds set on repeat or like droning airplanes. "I do not differentiate between sounds made by nature, sounds made by man, and sounds made by machines. I take it all in, Yen." Sometimes during dinner he became expansive. I was the only one to whom he could talk. Usually I had the whole house to myself in winter, but this year he was on sabbatical, woodshedding as he called it. Oh, Mr. Tinberg, I would like my house back. Although we both know that it is your house, every winter I think of it as mine. My two children grew up safely in this house, before leaving. One of them is in New York City—maybe you see him sometimes, though I doubt you would recognize him. The other is lost. I am like an old peasant in Vietnam, grown content with my daily walk to the store in town.

It is an old house but quite solid. It requires much maintenance, and I have learned to do things on my own without the help of local handymen, who are mostly thieves, too willing to take advantage of a woman they think knows nothing, not even the price of lumber or PVC. Tinberg showed up a week after they had all returned to New York City—Mr. Tinberg and his new young wife, Saraya, with her long blonde hair that instead of hiding its dark roots accentuates them, and their child, the baby Green, named after one of Mr. Tinberg's artist friends, a sculptor—he showed me pictures of "installments," a person must walk through the sculpture, whose walls veer and pitch and yaw. No, Mr. Tinberg, that is not for me. I will keep to my own way of seeing the world, thank you. The baby is becoming sweeter now but was so colicky at first; when they first arrived in summer the baby would wail through each night, keeping everyone awake. I could hear him even in the guesthouse down by the ocean, where I have my room in the summer. I like my room in the summer because of the ocean breeze, the long incoming waves, tides and tides, the rocky beach. This country and its landscape are still capable of surprising me with their beauty. I will look up at the green, the swaying grass in heavy wind, the sunrise over the ocean, and I will fill up like a balloon and almost lift off the ground. It is so different from the Vietnamese village in which I was born. Big changes are part of everyone's life now. Mr.

Tinberg returned to the house alone, and I thought he must have forgotten something, but then he carried many boxes inside—a turntable, a box of LPs, scores of his music, his computer system. "I am going to write my symphony here, Yen," he said. "This winter." "Haven't you already done that, Mr. Tinberg?" "No. Not this one. This is the big one. The real one." He was excited, as if all the music he had made before then had meant nothing. He has received honors and awards and his music is featured in many films—all of them the better sort—but he is still unhappy.

Often I think that Mr. Tinberg must be crazy. If someone were to test him they would find him to some degree or other insane, but if they were to medicate him against the effects of that mental illness he would lose his musical abilities. It is best to keep that madness hidden away, Mr. Tinberg. Broken to pieces, your gift means nothing. Although I do not think much of his music, I am aware that he is doing something that others are not. If there is a river that he taps into, as he claims, other musicians have not yet found it. When I was a young girl, my grandfather tried to show me how to play the flute, his old hands loose-skinned on the stops. "Like this, child." I have been here for so long that even my memories speak English. Awkward at first, with English, oh so horribly awkward, but over the years improving. Mr. Tinberg has a full library here and I read. There is not much to do in the winter but clean and keep the house up—at first it was even easier because the house was not so old then—and I would copy words out of books, some of them quite strange books. *Ferdydurke.* I copied *Ferdydurke* out word by word, tried to make sense of the words' strange arrangements. The man who becomes a child again. Dostoyevsky in translation, ancient Chinese poetry. Many things in translation. Sometimes I have gone for entire winter weeks without seeing anybody. Often, especially in the beginning, I did not speak to anyone for an entire winter. I would make lists and give the lists to Mr. Royles at the store, before he died, and he would fill my box with the items I needed and I would walk back up the road. When I had the children, I would take care of the children, too. They would go to school, come home, and I would help them with their homework. The so-quick progression from childhood to adulthood. By the time they were fourteen they no longer needed me. Cold, cold, always so cold.

The winter Mr. Tinberg came back was colder than ever. Walk out and the juice of your eyeballs freezes. Open your mouth and your spit freezes. Wind like a horrible tormenting animal out of the northeast, sometimes bringing snow, but, since we are so close to the ocean here, not snowing often. Usually the sky is merely gray, swept slate. "You don't mind that I'm here, do you, Yen?" We shared bottles of wine with dinner. Mr. Tinberg's corkscrew hair was still black, but his face was lined like the faces of old men, the pouches beneath the eyes sagging a bit further each year, jowls filling out. Last winter he had a cancerous growth removed from his neck and the skin grew back smooth and pink. Often, Mr. Tinberg had bad breath due to all the wine and because often he ate whole cloves of roasted garlic smeared on toast. While he was working in the upstairs studio, and sounds like strangled birds emerged from behind the closed door, I tidied his bedroom, which held in the scent of his night farts. The window had to be opened, a cold scourge on the wood floors. You could skate across them sometimes, they were so cold. Things were rotting inside his body. We are all aging. He took care of himself by doing Tai Chi in the morning, in sunlight on the odd occasions that there was any, his aging body bulky in loose black workout clothes. I would laugh at him if I did not know him. I kept healthy with my walks to the store and with work. There was wood that needed cutting, and every day I spent some time in the bracing cold wielding my ax. Work that was easy twenty, thirty years ago was now difficult. For entire weeks Mr. Tinberg did not leave the house. Behind his glasses, he stared out the window at the ocean.

"Why is this symphony so important?" I asked him over a simple meal of noodles and pork.

"This is the big one, Yen. This is what I've been working toward all my life. I can feel it coming." Sometimes, from behind the door, it sounded like a hundred violins all going at once, crazy crazy. Once, while I was carrying bedding down the hallway, I heard the most beautiful woman's voice repeating a simple melody line, and I stopped to listen. It was uncharacteristically beautiful, haunting, otherworldly, what have you. The hairs on my neck raised and tears built but did not fall from my eyes. Dumb dumb emotion. Again and again he played that melody with the woman's voice, the woman's voice so real that it seemed as if she were there but she wasn't, it was just his computer. Slowly he began removing notes from the melody. One after another the notes disappeared until only two notes remained and they sounded nothing like what I had heard before. The woman's voice became the blat of a French horn. Then it was swallowed inside sounds from all kinds of sources—machines and beating pans. Sometimes it seemed like childsplay, what Mr. Tinberg does, but often I heard that melody repeating in my mind. I lie awake at night listening to it run through the house. The house had soaked that melody into its wood. Such an old, good house. If you take care of something long enough it becomes a part of you, you become a part of it.

Every night just after dinner, as I was clearing the plates and cleaning the plates and drying the plates and returning the plates to their proper place in the cabinet, Mr. Tinberg called his wife and son on his cell phone. For some reason, he needed me there when he talked to them, needed me to listen in as he told his wife how his work was progressing— there was often nothing to tell—and listened to news of the city, asked about this or that person, expressed surprise or disappointment, laughed largely. Then he talked to his son in a higher kinder softer voice, telling him how much he loved and missed him and sleep well for daddy and dream about elephants and giraffes and I'll be seeing you before too long. Then, he would go to his room, I would go to my room, we would go back to our separate lives. I would call my son in New York City, ask if he'd heard anything from his sister. He never has. She could be anywhere or nowhere, dead or alive. When she became a teenager we struggled. She wanted more freedom. There was nothing to do here in this small town on this lonely island. She disappeared for days. I worried so much I nearly went crazy. She slipped away entirely. It's been years now. Living with Mr. Tinberg in the house was different, but I got used to it quickly, we all get used to everything so quickly.

We had been together for a long time, Mr. Tinberg and I, and he still found my hands remarkable. They were a working woman's hands, but they were not gnarled up, not yet. Many women my age suffer from arthritis, but my hands were strong and small and Mr. Tinberg watched me eat and smiled, as if it gave him pleasure just to watch me eating, maybe part of his fascination with the East and with Eastern ways of understanding. He tells me that he is working with Eastern scales in music, with microtones, but his music does not sound familiar to me, and I doubt it would sound familiar to anyone else, East or West. Usually when he worked he kept his music very quiet but sometimes it became very loud, filling the entire house, and in those times I had to leave, walk down the long road to the store, where they know me—the owner is the son of the former owner but the woman who is usually behind the counter is named Georgia. Georgia is large and loud, and I like her. I have always wondered why Mr. Tinberg is so interested in the East and yet all of his wives have been blonde and pretty and slight and last only a few years. This one has lasted the longest yet—she smells like baby oil and is kind to me, tries to treat me like something other than a servant. "He is playing his music loud again," I told Georgia, who grunted in reply, smiled and told me what to expect from the weather. Surprise, more cold, a storm coming next week. Some people are still not comfortable around me, there are not many foreigners here even now, but after so many years I have become a fixture, the one exception in their lives.

Mr. Tinberg was lying on the living room floor when I returned home from the store. He was wearing his jeans, a blue, ribbed cardigan sweater and his glasses, so I knew he was not doing Tai Chi or working out. He stretched himself out as long as he could and made a sound with his mouth, oh oh oh like a small sick dog. "What's wrong, Mr. Tinberg?" "My back," he said. "I threw my back out." "Doing what, writing music?" "Yes, writing music." For a moment or two he hated me, hated everything about me, blamed me, saw me as what I had always been, just a servant, a caretaker, someone to cook his favorite food in the summer and watch his property in the winter. A friend? Ha. A confidante? Never. "I don't know acupuncture," I said, "but I know massage. Take off your sweater and roll over." I warmed my hands and kneaded his muscles. He kept his undershirt on. Such pale fleshy skin, padded with subcutaneous fat. If he were not well-known in the music world he would not have been able to sleep with the young women he has. He is a difficult man, but they put up with him, loved him, pampered him. On the floor he was like a helpless child, moaning in pleasure and pain, like a piglet with pink skin, all of his muscles betraying tension. I had not touched a man so intimately since my husband died almost twenty years before. I straddled his large bottom and rode him, my small, facile hands on his blocky doughy skin. A little excitement, yes. A mild thrill. At that point I no longer masturbated, did not think of the body as a sexual thing anymore. That old life flared momentarily, died out, he put his shirt back on, I made us some tea and we sat on the living room floor together.

The sun was dying quickly, the wind pushing its way forcefully through the windowpanes, and it was the time for confessions, so Mr. Tinberg confessed. "I came here in part to get away from my son and my wife. Happy family life has always been difficult for me. I simply don't believe in it."

"Yes?" I said, presenting him with the face he wanted me to wear, the inchoate oriental, the unconditional therapist.

"Yes. Maybe because of my own past."

We all have our own pasts, Mr. Tinberg. I don't know yours, you don't know mine. Let's not start now. Let's just live here in this house that gets much too cold at night. I know you don't want me to warm you up at night, but I would be happy to slip into your bed momentarily, a fleeting glimpse of something that might have been.

"My own rotten childhood."

"Yes?" I said.

"This is wonderful tea," he said, holding the teacup in the palms of both hands. His hands were large and clumsy and smooth from not working. He looked around him, through the window at the sky bunching up with clouds. In *Ferdydurke*, the book I spent so long copying out, the book that helped me learn English, the narrator begins his story by walking under clouds shaped like buttocks, or maybe they actually are buttocks. He is an adult but he is forced to go back to his childhood, to those puerile desires and phobias and neuroses. Mr. Tinberg made a mighty effort to concentrate fully on everything that was happening at that moment, he attempted to really be present in the moment. "How are your children?" he asked. "Oh, they are fine, Mr. Tinberg," I replied. "Thank you for asking." Fine, except for the one who is missing. Except for my lost daughter. That night while I cried I heard that melody, the one he had stripped bare and then killed. I wanted to tell him that I had heard it, that he shouldn't have killed it, that he should bring it back to life. The house creaked, the wind pushed the windows like a large gray animal, the ocean seemed malevolent and all-swallowing, just out there, almost close enough to touch. The winter was not even half over yet.

ON THE NEXT MONDAY Mr. Tinberg took his car and vroomed off into the cold hills without a single word to me, and he returned with the singer woman. The singer woman was blonde and European, with long limbs, a long neck, hair that seemed like another part of her, something that followed her around dutifully. She handed me her coat upon arrival, and they sat near the fire in the living room and talked and talked while I cooked dinner, suddenly having to keep busy at all times because another person had invaded our winter solitude. Mr. Tinberg had long ago stopped paying any attention to what I did, but I felt that this woman would be watching me, that she had been raised to know how to handle servants. I started a stew that Mr. Tinberg liked and that would take a great effort to prepare, prepared homemade bread, braided, and tried not to listen to them. I felt that Mr. Tinberg was on the edge of a cliff, that he had not brought the singer woman here to help with his symphony, as he claimed, but for more prurient reasons, because she was striking and he was obviously smitten with her. He called her Analisa and laughed at her jokes.

We sat down to dinner, the three of us, which made the singer woman uncomfortable. She gave me glances, but Mr. Tinberg finally introduced us, calling me his caretaker. The stew was hearty and just right for the weather, which had turned colder and stormier. The woman looked out the window and shuddered.

"This is a horrible place, Robert," she said. "So cold, so desolate. I can see why you like it, though. It must be good for you, with your creative temperament. I couldn't stand it for long." "It's home," Mr. Tinberg said, smiling strangely. He had drunk too much wine, his face bloated. There was no phone call to Saraya and Green that night—instead, while I washed the dishes, they disappeared up to his studio. Not much later I heard her singing. I had hated her with all my being before I heard her singing, but it was beautiful singing, the same melody I had heard in the hallway before. I stopped what I was doing to listen. That melody touched parts of my body that had not been touched in years. It seemed to start in the chest and work its way outward to each of my limbs. One by one the notes were removed from the melody, until it became ugly and ordinary again. At the end she was droning two notes over and over again. I dried the dishes, put them away, wished the guesthouse was open, but it wasn't.

In my room I wrote a letter to my lost daughter, something I do regularly. I tell her that whatever she has done I forgive her and that if she just comes back and tells me she's okay she can do anything she wants. There had been tension, as there always is between mother and daughter, but I had no idea how much the tension hurt her. All of our children get lost, but not completely. Someday I still believed I would hear from her. The singer woman was singing various melodies against a background of strange noise. What had started as music had become a jumble of sounds. Why would he want to do that to beautiful music? I wrote a second letter to my son, in New York City, asking him how he was doing and telling him that Mr. Tinberg was back for the winter, about his symphony and about all that I had done to keep up the house. The two musicians worked well into the night. Mr. Tinberg was often obsessive about his work. He would work a problem out for hours, and then he would come crawling up out of these work sessions like a waking beast. Her voice was beautiful but not perfect or rounded. There was a little edge to it, the capacity to cut. I listened/didn't listen, lay in bed, finally falling asleep.

Most of Mr. Tinberg's summer guests, famous or not, would treat me like a human being. I was not another thing to them, but to the singer woman that was exactly what I was. She did not see me, even. She stood by the window in a thick turtleneck, tights, and a long skirt, and she shivered. She was ice, and Mr. Tinberg could be fire or he could become ice, as well. They drank a good deal and laughed even more, but there didn't seem to be anything physical between them. I would have heard them in the night. Maybe it was just the sense of tension, the constant possibility that Mr. Tinberg liked. "Doesn't she have remarkable hands, Analisa?" "They are just hands, Robert." "But look at them." "Mmm." When he finally did call his wife and child, he made up some excuse, he barked at her. He was often difficult, and now was his time to be difficult. Too much time indoors, too much work, too much concentrated in his head. I could feel the energy coiled inside him. He prowled the downstairs rooms, banged things around.

"I could lose everything and not even care," Mr. Tinberg said at dinner one night. He held his wine glass, fingers splayed out. "I could lose *everything* and not even care." He looked at each of us in turn, challenging us.

"What is there to lose, Robert?" the singer woman asked.

"Everything."

"Hmmm," she grinned. She wore a white turtleneck, no bra. She ate men for a hobby. "I thought everything was an illusion. Isn't that what your Buddhism says?" "Everything is suffering. But suffering can be overcome." He wanted to tip over the edge of a cliff and fall, but the singer woman would not let him. I cleared the plates, I washed the plates, I put the plates back in their proper place.

Then, one night a few days after the singer woman had arrived, I woke and went to my window. The moon had woken me, bright bright, cold cold. A cone of moonlight stood still on the ocean. Looking down at the unkempt lawn leading to the rocky beach, I was surprised to see the singer woman, even more surprised to see that she was not wearing any clothes. Her skin was as white as alabaster, her nipples were large and purple, her hair was pale, and she was staggering, drunk. She appeared to be lost. It was difficult to see her face from that distance, but I imagined her with open mouth and open eyes. You should help her, Yen, a voice inside me said. You should go out there with a warm blanket and guide her back inside.

Instead, after a few minutes, I went back to my bed, and in the morning I was not at all sure whether what I had seen was a dream or not. Mr. Tinberg sat at the kitchen table, his head heavy. "She's gone," he said. "She left this morning. I drove her to the ferry. I will never finish it." "You will finish it, Mr. Tinberg," I said, watering a fern by the side window. The full moon had swept everything clear. The tall grass was gold in the bright sun. He disappeared into his room and did not come out for two days. I imagined him inside the room, pulling his entrails out. Where was his hidden river now?

He finished his symphony, of course. Within those two days he finished it. Two days later he sat on the couch in a forest green shirt and said to me, "Yen, it's strange, but I actually miss my family." He returned to them and performed the symphony in several cities with a number of singers— never with one named Analisa. The melody lasted for five seconds of the symphony, but it was the best thing he had ever done. He has never wintered in Nova Scotia again. I have not heard from my daughter yet, but my son calls me every week. When I walked to the store later that day, after I had seen the singer woman in the night, I felt it, just a drop, a taste, a touch—winter would be over in a few weeks. There would be much work to do. The guesthouse would have to be cleaned. The wood floors would need to be refinished. I went to the hardware store and looked at belt-sanders. I would buy kneepads and a facemask and get down there and work and work. I was almost giddy with the prospect.

K9

His buddies from the force gave him the dog when they came over to play poker and get drunk. It was a retired K9, Jose's partner for ten years. "He's a good old dog," Jose said, scratching the dog behind the ear. "I love this dog. And it's a perfect match. You need something to get your ass off the couch; he needs to retire."

His buddies had been coming over to play poker once a week since John had fallen from the roof of his split entry house, where he'd lived with Gaby before she left him. He'd been cleaning out the gutters in the fall. It was something he'd done every year for seven years, no problem. He still wasn't sure what went wrong. His boot slipped on the top rung of the aluminum ladder as he was climbing down, and he felt himself fall. God, he hated that feeling. The complete loss of control. Landing, he'd jammed his leg so bad white and shiny bone stuck out of the skin. At first it hadn't hurt, but then it hurt like a motherfucker, almost as bad as when he'd been shot in Vineland his second day on the job, the only time in his career he'd been shot. Pain radiated up from his leg like slow flames. He'd had to crawl into the house to get his cell phone, grappling up the stairs once he was in the house, leaving behind a slime trail of blood.

The pain had been intense, and he knew it would take time to recuperate, but he hadn't expected it to knock him off the force altogether. Even six months after the accident he could barely walk. He rarely left his house, because the seven steps leading to the front door were too daunting. He never went downstairs into the basement, with the big screen TV, the built-in bar, the pool table, and the weight set anymore. His buddies told him they were going to build him a ramp inside the house or get him a stairlift, but so far they hadn't and he wasn't about to bug them about it. He hated charity.

When Jose told him he was gifting him the dog, John looked at the K9, a purebred German Shepherd, and shook his head.

"Nuh-uh," he said. "I don't even like dogs."

"Fuck you, man. Everyone likes dogs."

"Not me. I don't like dogs."

"Boolshit."

And they had kept on playing poker.

They played for small money. Mostly it was an excuse to get trashed. They talked about things that had happened to them out on their beats. Sean was a homicide detective, but Jose and Frank and the kid, Troy, patrolled. They were all tough, meatheaded guys. John had played high school football against Frank—he played for Vineland; Frank played for Buena—and they joked about the rivalry all the time. They both still went to high school games sometimes. They were all Eagles fans. E.A.G.L.E.S.

John had nothing to add to the conversations anymore. He had no stories to tell, unless they were stories from the past, and everyone had heard those stories a thousand times already. The time he walked into an apartment after a call to find a woman trapped under a fat man who'd had a heart attack while he was fucking her. The way she wheezed out "hheeellp." The school shooting he helped quash. They told him about the latest boneheaded decision Chief DeAngelis had made and talked about the lowlifes and degenerates everyone knew, this dealer or that rat, and it gave John a mild sense of belonging, but ever since the accident he'd felt himself winging away from everything. He barely knew who he was anymore.

The injury gave him time, way too much time, to think about Gaby, who'd left him after seven years of what he thought was a perfectly decent marriage.

He didn't like to think.

He watched a lot of TV and tried to read thrillers. Sometimes the plots got away from him, and he would bull through, page after page of descriptions that didn't add up to anything.

His biceps and pecs and back, which he'd spent years developing and strengthening, lifting for at least an hour and a half every day, sometimes two or more hours, were going soft, bloated.

The only thing he kept from his time on the force was his haircut, a buzz cut he maintained himself. He knew he was not cut out for a desk job, and that disability would only last so much longer.

Throughout that first night that they gave him the dog, John kept looking at the dog, and the dog kept looking back at him. It'd sniffed around the whole upstairs of the house for ten minutes when they first brought him in, as if trying to see if the place was up to snuff, then he settled down on the couch in a tawny ball. John wanted to yell at him to get off the couch, but he looked comfortable, and what the hell.

When the men left, half or three quarters drunk, sloppy, the dog stood at attention. He watched Jose leave with a kind of rigid wariness, and he started whining as soon as Jose was out the door. The whining lasted about fifteen minutes, fifteen excruciating minutes of dog crying before he lowered his head onto the floor and looked sad. While John watched TV, another cop show, this one set in LA, the dog would look up now and then.

He closed the bedroom door that night and heard the dog's nails clicking on the Pergo floor. He really didn't like dogs. As a kid he'd begged and pleaded his parents to let him get a dog, but they refused. They moved around a lot because his father was in the Army, and it would have been irresponsible to get a dog. He figured he'd passed some threshold—after a while dog ownership stopped making sense. He got sick of seeing people walking their dogs everywhere. Gaby had wanted a dog, too, but he'd put his foot down. She'd wanted some kind of little crossbred puppy, a cockapoo or something. No thanks. He knew he should have let her get it. If he'd let her get it maybe she would have stayed with him. He thought that about every little thing now, though. If he had just done this or if he had just done that, maybe she would have stayed. The truth was: there was no keeping Gaby.

In the morning the dog followed him into the kitchen and watched him while he got out the bowl and food Jose had left. The dog seemed to have a kind of intelligence John didn't expect out of a dog. He seemed more watchful than a normal dog. John wondered what was going on behind those gigantic brown eyes. He'd probably seen some shit. *Me, too, buddy,* he almost said.

Right after eating, the dog stood at the back sliding doors and barked. The doors looked out onto the overgrown backyard and beyond that to the woods, thick pine barrens. When John forced himself up and pulled open the sliders, the dog took off like a brown and black rocket, slithering down the stairs and toward the pines. Maybe it wouldn't come back, he half-hoped. He sat down, ate his cereal, drank his coffee, scrolled around on his phone. The dog came back an hour later.

It was a matter of accommodation. He had to accommodate himself to the dog, and the dog had to accommodate itself to him. He had never understood this aspect of pet ownership before. Why would someone want to have something they had to take care of, something so needy? The dog seemed to miss his time on the force, miss driving around with Jose, sniffing out drugs, doing whatever it was that K9s did. John missed his job, too, the strung tension of it. Every time you left the house you weren't sure what was going to happen, if you were going to come back the same way you left, if you were going to come back at all. Something could pop off at any moment. Now nothing was going to pop off all day.

He turned on the TV at noon and watched the news a while, switching between Fox and CNN. Things were going nuts out in the world. The pandemic was *still* going on. It was easy to forget the pandemic was happening when he hardly left his house—he got his food delivered, making the arduous voyage down the stairs to fetch the boxes about once a week—but on the news there were all these images of people wearing masks and waiting in lines to get tested. There were cellphone videos of antivaxxers and antimaskers going nuts in public places. His buddies on the force were mostly antivaxxers, or they didn't talk about it at all. My body, my choice motherfucker. John had already had the 'rona, a two-week ordeal where he hacked up his lungs and couldn't smell anything. He knew it was real.

He called his parents down in Florida and talked to his mother for a while.

Nothing was new with them.

Nothing was ever new with them. His father was retired. Both of them were healthy.

Around three o'clock the dog started barking, and John looked out the window to see a group of neighborhood kids cutting through his backyard, the way they always did. There were about five of them, and about two were Hispanic. They were all between eight and twelve years old, if he had to guess. They cut through the yard every school day. It gave him something to look forward to. Sometimes they wrestled each other, sometimes they threw little sticks at each other. He looked out and saw one of them, a young dark-haired kid about ten years old, looking up at the sliders, probably noticing the dog going nuts.

By the time Jose and them came back for the next poker night, John and the dog had accommodated themselves to each other. He kept the bedroom door open at night. He didn't admit it to himself, but he hoped the dog would jump up into the bed with him, and after a while it did. It curled up beside him, this warm comfortable breathing shape. It was a kind of relief. It was almost like the ghost of Gaby come back to comfort him. She was gone, gone, gone. Sometimes he went onto her Facebook page to see the pictures she posted of her new family in Philadelphia. Her husband, who was somehow both a geologist and a punk rock musician, a skinny black dude he wouldn't trust with anything. Their kid. Their nice house. He wanted to smash it all, but the injury made that a pipe dream. He tried not to think about it.

His buddies ragged on him about how much he liked the dog and how much the dog obviously liked him. He'd greeted Jose warmly, but then he curled up beside John's chair. They told John he seemed happier, thinner even, now. He didn't believe them, but he smiled sheepishly. "Whatever," he said.

Winter turned to spring, and sometimes he'd watch the kids returning from school with mud on their boots. He watched the buds of trees pop at the ends of branches. He noticed things he'd never noticed before. He still spent a lot of time sitting in front of the TV, but he also spent a lot of time at the kitchen table now, looking out, vaguely planning out the rest of his life. If he couldn't go back to the force, at least not on patrol, he had to figure out what he was going to do with his life. The idea of not being a cop scared the shit out of him, but he had no desire for a desk job and knew he couldn't do it well. They'd probably give him a pity job, something he couldn't fuck up too badly, but he had liked being a cop, liked being good at something. He'd been a natural, with good instincts. He slipped into little fantasies. Maybe he'd become an elementary school teacher. The idea was so preposterous he almost spit out his coffee the first time he thought it, but what if… He pictured himself in front of a class of thirty third graders. In the fantasy, they listened to him.

With a feeling of shame, the way he used to look at porn when Gaby was around, though there was no one to hide anything from now, he started searching out programs at local schools. The community college was less than a mile from his house. He had nothing but a high school diploma. When he'd graduated, he thought college was not for him, that he was too dumb for it, but he wasn't really dumb. There were dumber motherfuckers than him with full-on graduate degrees. Why not? He dared to dream.

He started walking out onto the deck whenever he let the dog outside. There was a spate of days in the 80s, days so warm clouds of gnats congregated everywhere. He made his way down the stairs of the back deck, slowly. He still couldn't put weight on his leg and used his crutches everywhere he went. Soon, if he worked on it, he'd be able to walk without the crutches. He'd lurch everywhere. He ruffed the dog around the neck and threw an old tennis ball for it to fetch. The dog was old but still had energy. There was life in the old boy yet.

JOHN FORCED HIMSELF OUT to his old truck, pulled himself up into the cab, and drove to PetSmart to get the dog a toy and some food. It was the first time he'd driven anywhere since the accident, but the dog deserved it. He wore the mask he'd bought early on in the pandemic. People looked at him funny, and he looked back at them funny. It was like living on the goddamn moon. He didn't like it at all. It was better to stay holed up in his split-entry. Better to never come out at all. But the dog—he'd started calling it Chief, because it reminded him a little of DeAngelis, his old boss—loved the hard red rubber ball he bought it. He worked his teeth against it, growling happily.

Everything was getting better. It was not perfect, because nothing was ever perfect, but things were improving. He took a placement test online for the community college and registered for an English class in the fall. He both dreaded it and looked forward to it. It would be something different, at least. When they watched cop shows, he and Chief both considered them with a critical eye. If that were me… If I were in that situation… That's bullshit, that would never happen… He patted the dog's side and they exchanged glances.

He guessed it was a kind of love.

THEY MUST HAVE BEEN LET OUT early from school. He never let Chief out when the kids were walking through his backyard. He wasn't stupid. But as he sat at the kitchen table at about eleven o'clock, the dog outside doing his business, he heard a commotion from the yard: yelling followed by screaming. A piercing scream. He'd heard screams like that several times in his line of work before. Screams of pain mixed with horror. When he looked out the window, he saw them all gathered together in a clump. At first he couldn't tell what was happening. There was a lot of brown and a lot of black, with the dead leaves and the mud, and the kids wore black and brown clothing, and the dog was black and brown, but after a couple seconds the scene focused in for him. Chief had his teeth clamped onto a little boy's arm. It was the little boy that was screaming.

John couldn't run, but he moved as quickly as he could, clomping his bad foot down like a club, throwing open the sliders. Throughout his years on the force, he'd learned to regulate adrenaline, to funnel it to the proper places. His eyesight grew sharp. His critical faculties heightened.

"Chief!" he yelled, but the dog ignored him, growling deep in his throat. One of the kids had picked up a thick branch and was whacking the dog's head with it. "Ho!" he called, to the dog, to the boy with the branch, to all of them. He already had a sense that everything in his life had changed. Again. "Ho!"

When he was close enough, he could see the growling dog's eyes and its sharp brownish teeth. It had become an engine of pure menace. A malevolent thing. John thought about how he'd pictured Satan back when he was a kid, when his parents would take him to the chapel at whatever base they were on. He'd always imagined a being like this: pure evil. The muscles of the dog's face were pulled back taut. There was blood. The kid with the branch caught the dog on the head with a solid whack while another one poked it in the stomach with a second, sharper branch, and the dog was surprised and released the boy's arm. The dog rocketed off into the woods, the kids ran the other way, and John Navarro was left alone in his backyard.

He waited for the dog to return, but he didn't. After a while John walked back into his house, clomping up the stairs. His leg throbbed painfully. It'd been stupid to put so much weight on it. The adrenaline had made him careless. It'd been stupid to accept the dog in the first place. He should have known better. Something like this had been bound to happen. That was the kind of luck he had. The house felt so empty without Chief, though. John wondered if he should call animal control, but if he did he might lose the dog. He waited for his neighbors to come, knock on his door, and give him hell. He was going to get sued, for sure—unless they were undocumented. A better man than John would have gone over and made sure the kid was alright. He could see the boy's arm, the meat of his muscles rending. He was pretty sure he'd seen bone. That kid was going to be frightened of dogs the rest of his life. And where was the dog? Chief was out there in the pine barrens now, roaming, maybe hunting. Maybe he was biting every kid in the little South Jersey town. Wreaking havoc. He imagined a scene out of a monster movie, the military lining up behind big guns to blow the dog away.

It was about eight o'clock and he was watching Fox News when he heard scraping at the back door. The dog had learned how to request to come in, politely, by scraping the door once with his paw, a sound that had become part of John's everyday life. Relief settled inside him like something melting. The dog looked so sweet and harmless waiting to be let in it was hard to believe what he'd done.

He let the dog curl up onto the couch with him. He gave him extra treats. When they went to bed, he put his arm around the breathing body of the dog. The dog was better than a wife. More loyal and less questioning. But ultimately no less risky.

In the morning he made eggs and bacon, and he set down a plate for himself and a plate on the floor for the dog. Chief looked up at him with deep gratitude in his eyes and tucked in with a kind of pleasure that people could never experience.

He dressed and put his holster on, the service revolver he hadn't touched since the accident. Sense memories flooded him when he touched it. Sometimes nothing would happen. A day could pass without incident. But more often something would pop off. Domestic disturbances, often. The world was more fucked up than most people realized. Most people lived on the surface, but under the surface some deep and rotten shit was rolling around at all times. He'd seen kids starved almost to the point of death. He'd seen women who'd been raped and murdered. It had all done a number on him. *That* was why Gaby left him.

He led the dog out to the truck. It was slow going. He might have reinjured his leg the day before, trying to get Chief to stop biting the kid. It hurt worse than ever. The dog hopped up into the truck, probably remembering hopping into the patrol car with Jose back when he was a K9. They both had their training. Neither of them could really change all that much.

He drove out of town, deeper into the pinelands. When John first moved to South Jersey the pinelands horrified him, they were so endless. It had been easy to imagine the Jersey Devil actually existed, something as evil as that. The trunks of the trees were all bare, any foliage they had fifty feet in the air. The ground was padded with pine needles. It went on forever. After a few years, John had grown to appreciate the pinelands. He grew to like driving or hiking through them. He came to understand them, in a way. He'd hunted for a few years with buddies from the force, picking off deer that existed in copious numbers, sometimes goose hunting from blinds. They were members of the same gun clubs. After a childhood spent moving around, John had been happy to settle down here. He'd expected to have kids with Gaby and raise them right, but somehow they drifted apart. She met her current husband while she was at a fundraiser for her job in Philly, where she was the managing editor of a fitness magazine. She and John bonded because of their love of working out, but he had never been able to give her what she wanted. She had done him wrong, and he was still proud of the fact that he hadn't killed the motherfucker, the way he'd wanted to, the way he'd planned to.

He pulled the truck down the narrow dirt road only a select few knew about and drove several miles, then took an even smaller dirt road off the first dirt road. He remembered the last time he'd driven out here, the kid literally shaking in the cruiser beside him. The kid was a degenerate. A wastoid. Tattoos ran up and down his arms and covered his neck, two wings feathering out around his Adam's apple. A teardrop below his eye. He was tall and stringy. It had been the middle of summer. Almost a hundred degrees. There had been heatwaves out the window in the distance.

Now it was a beautiful spring day, and the dog stuck his head out the open window of the truck, his tongue waving in the wind. He looked more like a pup than like a killer dog.

John pulled into the clearing beside the dirt road he'd helped clear years ago. There was new growth, but the truck slotted right into the space. When he opened the passenger side door, he told the dog to run. Not out loud, but in his head. *Run,* he thought. *Run, motherfucker.* But the dog got out and walked slowly right beside him.

He'd pulled the degenerate out of the cruiser. When the dude's knees buckled, he dragged him, feeling the handcuffs dig into the dude's wrists. He had been in his prime then, and it was no thing to drag the guy after him. Easy peasy. Finally the fucker found his feet, and John pushed him ahead, into the dark hot pinelands. They had both started sweating almost immediately. Navarro could smell piss. The fucker had pissed himself.

Run, he thought, but the dog didn't go more than ten feet from him before sauntering back to his side. The dog sniffed the depression in the ground, where John had buried the fucker. It had been three years ago, right before Gaby left him. He didn't question his decision. The degenerate had not deserved to live. If John had let him go to trial, he probably would have got off, got out, been a waste of space, done more damage to the world. Chief sniffed eagerly at the ground, and he looked up at John just as John was extending his arm, bracing himself for the recoil of the service revolver.

The Blue of Broken Bones

Cynthia slid into the driver's seat of her Volvo, sat looking at the house. Although daylight saving time had not yet ended, the days were already shorter, closing like shutters. It was evening, and there were people inside her house drinking wine and eating food others had brought. Her parents were inside, her father dressed in his best black suit, her mother in a black wrap dress. Her husband. They were either talking or assiduously not talking about her murdered daughter. Amelia.

After returning from the funeral, Cynthia had changed into black jeans and a baggy University of New Hampshire sweatshirt, trading pumps for canvas sneakers. She'd washed her face and drunk two glasses of wine, the first slipping down easily but the second threatening to back up on her. The wine "went right to her head," as people said. She had nibbled on raw vegetables, a slice of crusty bread smeared with pesto.

Anyone passing on the road below would think the McCraes were having a party. In two weeks it would be Thanksgiving. And what were they supposed to do then? How were they supposed to live through that? She opened the glove compartment, pulled out maintenance receipts for the Volvo, records of brake and transmission repairs, receipts for every oil change, the user's manual, until she found it, shoved in the back: the crumpled soft-pack of generic cigarettes she'd stowed there when she was quitting. She slid one of the three remaining cigarettes out of the pack. It glowed in the dark of the car's interior like a small bone. She lit it with a match, the book from her purse, the soft sulfur head popping reluctantly to life.

She did not open the windows but let the smoke layer itself in the air around her, putting her in mind of scenes from movies, the suicide in the garage. She put the key in the ignition and turned it, headlights flooding the out-building where Amelia's bike still hung from hooks. There were old photographs of her inside there, old boxes full of crafts she'd made in school, projects and drawings that had embarrassed the almost-grown Amelia but were so damned sweet. Cynthia was tempted to put the car in drive and ram the building, but that would eradicate nothing. She would have to burn the structure to the ground. Not even that would do any good.

She took a drag of the cigarette and put the Volvo in reverse, the transmission clunking into gear beneath her. The car was old and would not hold out much longer. She reversed down the long driveway, waiting for someone to come running out of the house to stop her. Cars were parked on the grass beside the driveway, her parents', her husband's parents', Diane's, Ellen from the bookstore's. No one emerged from the house. She found herself reversing onto the road, pointing the car toward 101, then driving onto 101, west. The road was long, straight, and dark, white crosses commemo-rating fatalities illuminated by her headlights. She counted a half dozen, some bare, some with impromptu memorials, stuffed bears and plastic flowers, before she stopped counting.

When she hit 93, she merged onto the ramp for the south interstate. The lights from other cars moved through the smoke trapped in the car, which eventually settled.

EVERY MILE WAS AN OPPORTUNITY to return to the house on the hill where her parents and husband mourned her daughter. She could explain that she'd needed to clear her head, and now that she'd done that she could face them again. But the truth was: her head was already clear, and she wasn't sure she could ever face them again. Every mile she rejected the opportunity to turn around, until it became impossible, until it was past midnight and she was still driving, now in western Massachusetts, on the turnpike. She was not tired. She didn't need to stop. She kept driving into New York. There was little to see out the windows, only trees and hills, trees and hills. Trucks shared the road with her, appearing as small white lights in her rearview, growing to the size of intense stars before passing, their drafts pressing against the side of the boxy Volvo. She held the wheel steady, hands at ten and two.

A few hours later she lit another cigarette, opened the window. The cool air smelled of earth. She tasted water in it, a lake, maybe. There were no stars. The second cigarette tasted as bad as the first, but this time she pulled the smoke deep into her lungs.

WHEN LIGHT STARTED SEEPING UP out of the ground, a dull roseate haze, she pulled off the thruway. She stopped at a Shell station, lit up in the predawn, filled the tank, bought a carton of Marlboro Lights, the brand she'd smoked as a teenager, a small bottle of orange juice, some trail mix in a plastic pouch. She sat in the car chomping almonds, shelled candies and raisins, washing it down with the juice, rose turning gray around her. She thought of flowers blooming and dying.

She drove away from the highway until coming to a wooden sign for a lake. She pulled into a little park near the lake, parked the car in an empty dirt lot. She could feel the smoke in her lungs, the food in her stomach. The lack of sleep. The weight of dead dreams. Ted would be worried about her, and she didn't like to worry him, but calling him now…she couldn't. She didn't.

She watched a pickup truck appear in her rearview mirror and back up, pointing the simple metal rowboat it towed toward the water, a boy, maybe ten, getting out to direct the driver. The boy wore a flannel shirt and a dark vest with small quilted sections. A cowlick stood up on the back of his head. When the boat was near the water, he took it off the hitch and pulled it into the lake. The man came around to help. They placed a cooler and two fishing rods into the boat. The man carried a thermos. Wisps on the lake's surface were like the smoke inside the car. The man parked the truck and came loping back, and he and the boy launched the boat, rowing, the oars clanking against oarlocks, the sound of water moving against the paddles strangely musical.

Cynthia lowered the seatback all the way and curled onto her side. She could see the gray trees in her periphery, could hear birdsong. She closed her eyes and fell asleep.

WHEN SHE GOT OUT OF THE CAR, the sky was half cleared. Wind had pushed away the wall of dark clouds, revealing a washed-out blue. A family had claimed a picnic area to her right and children were yelling, chasing each other, adults setting up camp. A young couple walked past holding hands. Cynthia stretched before walking toward the lake. It was small, a mile or so in diameter, and she could see the rowboat in the distance, two fishing poles raised. She walked the perimeter trail around the lake. When a little path broke off, she walked to the shore. Roots grew into the lake, thick and broken by perspective where they entered the water, reminding her of broken bones. She stepped onto a flat granite boulder by the water, sat down. It was warm now, the sun having emerged from the cloud cover. She took off her sweatshirt. Underneath, she wore an old My Chemical Romance concert t-shirt Amelia had worn so often it was paper thin in sections, gray at the underarms and around the neck. She had found the t-shirt in Amelia's closet, underneath other dirty clothes. The shirt had not been worn for years, but it still smelled of Amelia. She had been at her most distant then. Cruel and angry. Cynthia had not blamed her; adolescence was not easy for anyone. Rage against… everything. The shirt fit tight around the chest and was too short, some of her middle-aged belly puffing out between it and the waist of her jeans. She put the sweatshirt back on, not caring that it made her too hot.

HER HEAD, THOUGH CLEAR, could not figure anything out. She walked around the lake, stepping over fallen tree trunks with moss on their backs, rousting birds and squirrels. Three ravens perched on the same dead tree beside the lake. She could see the father and son fishing on the far side of the lake. They didn't speak but appeared content. She heard someone laughing when she was three quarters around the lake but didn't see the laugher. She was sweating, her chest tight, beads sliding down the small of her back. She was there in her body, tired, a sleep debt she wasn't sure she could ever repay, her lungs questioning her decision to smoke, her stomach unhappy with the trail mix and orange juice. She was her body only.

When she came back to her Volvo, she got out the trail mix and the rest of the orange juice and sat at the foot of a tree eating and drinking, watching the washed-out sky, no clouds now, reflected, stretched, in the lake. She thought of the small manmade pond in which her daughter's body had been found, the old barn falling down beside it where something too horrible to imagine had occurred. The autopsy report. She thought about getting up and looking at herself in the mirror of the lake's surface but knew what she would see. Didn't need to see it again. She hated herself for what she was doing but didn't know what that was yet.

When she got back into the car, she was not sure whether she would return or not, but when she approached the turnpike, she headed west.

WAITING IN A LONG LINE OF CARS at the Canadian border, Cynthia rummaged inside her purse. Of course she didn't have her passport. She had not been planning on leaving the country. They would turn her back and she would have to return to Ted, to New Hampshire, her life, which now seemed removed, something she would have to step back into, carefully. It would fit her imperfectly at first, the way Amelia's t-shirt fit her too tightly around the chest, but she would stretch it to accommodate her, or she would have to shrink to accommodate it. Around her were trucks and families on vacation, though not many because it was November. Commuters and commercial vehicles. She passed a woman driving a small black car wearing a hijab, her face so pretty it seemed carved. She passed a car full of people talking and laughing. She passed a man with slicked back hair in a luxury car. The line moved slowly.

When she approached the gate, she told the officer inside that her purpose was recreation. She opened her wallet and found her license. "Passport?" he asked. He was young and looked tired. It was strange how many people looked young to her now; doctors, her daughter's teachers, people on the news, they all looked like children. "Birth certificate?" he asked. She found the folded piece of paper in a compartment of her wallet, handed it to him. He unfolded and read it. "Have a good day," he said, handing her back the birth certificate.

She drove across a bridge that did not seem like a bridge, in another country. She drove for a long time before pulling off the highway at a shopping plaza. She walked into a small restaurant where everyone was white, ordered breakfast from a waitress in a brown uniform, ate eggs and hash browns, looking out at the highway. She didn't particularly want to eat, but she ate anyway. A young girl with long black hair sat with her parents. She was pale and looked sickly, but she smiled at something the father said, showing imperfect white teeth. Cynthia tipped the waitress too much then walked across the lot to a sporting goods store, where she bought a backpack with an aluminum frame, not top-of-the-line but quality, some packages of dried food, a cook set, a small propane stove, a zero-degree sleeping bag, a one-person tent, a package of fire starters, some matches. She tried on boots and bought the second most expensive pair. She bought four liters of water at the counter. When she handed across her credit card, she thought about Ted, tracking her movements. He'd know she was alive, in Canada. He would not pursue her, would wait for her to return. Maybe she would.

SHE SEEMED TO REMEMBER THE WAY. She had been ten when her parents brought her here for a camping trip. Her father's brother and his family, her two cousins, her aunt, lived in Toronto. Still. She could visit them if she wanted to. After spending a week in the city, seeing the sights, the CN Tower, the aquarium, they had traveled into the wilderness. She had prayed to see a bear. She'd fantasized about the bear recognizing her as someone special. She'd been fascinated with animals, had wanted to do something with them for a job, at first imagining becoming a veterinarian, the way children did, then imagining studying them or training them. She'd had an enormous collection of stuffed animals, proudest of the most unusual, the narwhal, the platypus. Her parents had indulged her, spoiled her, thinking it was the American way.

The Algonquin Provincial Park was the size of Connecticut. She drove down long empty roads, taking smaller and smaller roads, as if she knew where she was going, the Volvo handling the terrain with an animal stolidity. She avoided places where tourists might go, found herself driving down a long logging road that turned into an overgrown path, just wide enough for the Volvo, the scraping of weeds against the chassis. She pulled off the trail in the lee of two trees, got out and finished packing the backpack. The aluminum frame kept the weight off her back so it felt light, a reassuring pressure rather than a burden.

She looked back at the car once, shining silver in the sun, seeming out of place. How would she find it when she came back? Maybe she wouldn't. There was a high whine of insects. Within minutes she was hot and wished she'd taken off her sweatshirt, but she let herself sweat rather than take the pack off again.

SHE COULD NOT REMEMBER THE LAST TIME she'd been alone for so long. Maybe when Ted had gone on a camping trip with college friends, though then there had been Amelia. There was always someone. Family, students, colleagues. She was alone much of the time, in her office at the university or at home, but was rarely alone alone. The space inside her mind expanded. She wasn't thinking about preparing a lecture or reviewing a student's thesis or pursuing tenure, keeping up with the work in her field, MLA and Digital Humanities, wasn't worried about the news, the election of a billionaire megalomaniac to the presidency. All of this had been set to the side, leaving nothing. Her mind as blank as the landscape.

She happened onto a trail with purple blazes that took her up a mountain. By late afternoon, she was at the rim of a ravine, picking along the tree line, Lilliputian shrubs at her feet. The new boots already felt worn in. Her sweat dried in the cold wind, and she descended until she found a flat enough space by the side of the trail, a clearing nestled inside trees where someone before her had camped. She set up the tent and gathered dead wood. It looked like there had been a recent wildfire. She found stones and built a firepit, set a cube of fire starter inside, waited until night to light it.

SHE BOILED A CUP OF WATER on the little propane stove, filled a plastic packet with water and stirred, waited for the mixture to cool, then ate. She lit the fire when it was fully dark. She guessed it was around eight o'clock. Maybe later. The fire caught then died, and she didn't bother to light it again. Took off all her clothes, slid naked into her sleeping bag in the tent and fell asleep. At first she was too warm, but when she woke later the air around her was frigid and she could see her breath. She zipped the bag around her head like a mummy and breathed slowly, her eyes wide open. She remembered how her daughter felt, an infant at her side, the warmth of her, the weight like her own body returning to her. How painful but exhilarating the separation. How strange to hear her speak her first words, to process the world on her own, her strange mind blooming. How exasperating it could be when she became a teenager at eleven years old, much too early. That attitude. It could be funny, but it could also cut. How large and how jagged her love. She wished she could cry, but there were obstacles to her tears. There was anger she hadn't let herself feel yet right at the edge of things. How could Amelia be so stupid to get mixed up with someone who could do this to her? And who had done it? How could anyone?

How she wished she could believe in God at this moment, someone or something, even someone or something that could allow this to happen, who could take this burden from her, unravel it from her body. She pictured her grief like a long black snake coiled inside her, something that would come out of her mouth and stretch across the mountaintops. Miles of black writhing body. She was dreaming.

IN THE MORNING she headed deeper into the wilderness, up the ridge and past the tree line. Her body missed caffeine, her routine, but she ignored her body. She hiked with her daughter's t-shirt on, her bare arms cold at first, gooseflesh until her body warmed to moving. She felt like she could hike for days without tiring. And maybe she would.

As she walked, she imagined cutting off all her hair, collecting it in a ball and burning it. Wandering the mountains like a monk on a pilgrimage until the grief wore out. If it ever did. There were Korean mourning customs she didn't know or understand. She thought of Buddhist pilgrims prostrating themselves across mountains.

She imagined turning a corner on the trail and finding herself face-to-face with a black bear. The bear would open his enormous mouth, and she would walk inside his body. She would curl up inside his stomach for years, then she would stand and look through his eyes. She would lumber through this landscape, foraging, in fear sometimes, in kingly prepossession at other times. She would walk the rivers, swiping at salmon as they ran upstream, opening them with a razor-sharp claw.

The second night she set up camp miles from her first camp, looking out over a vast landscape. She saw no sign of human habitation, though she suspected it was there. An eagle rode wind currents. She ate her first meal of the day, built a small fire that flapped like a shirt, survived the cold night. Her water was already nearly gone.

SHE SAW THE FIGURE APPROACHING from a distance. The bulky pack on his back. His steady progress. She assumed he would take another trail, and they would not have to pass one another, but after an hour she saw him approaching down a wooded path between peaks. He wore a red bandana, was not as young as he appeared at first but was younger than her. A regular hiker. A man of the mountains.

"Fair warning. There's a bear down there," he said, smiling and gesturing behind him. His skin coated in sweat. She saw the spot on his neck where he usually shaved, red and irritated.

"Where?"

"By the lake. Be careful. I think there's a cub down there, too. I didn't see it, but I could hear it." Filled with the experience. Exhilarated.

She nodded and continued on. She heard the man start walking after a brief pause, as if he'd expected her to keep talking with him.

SHE SAW THE LAKE FROM A DISTANCE but didn't see any bears. At first she saw no sign of bears, but then she saw some scat and, a little farther on, a perfect paw-print in mud. She crouched and placed her hand into the heart of the paw-print. The paw was two times the size of her hand. The lake was nestled between the peaks and would catch sunlight for another hour before it was in shadow.

When she reached the shore, she took off the pack and placed it to the side, took off her boots and socks, her bare feet cold against the stone, took off her pants and underpants, Amelia's t-shirt. Gooseflesh. She felt old in a timeless way, as if she could slough off this skin, but also ridiculous. No one could see her, aside from the bears if they were around, but she felt as if she were acting. When she stepped into the lake, meeting her reflection, as if entering herself more fully, she gasped but didn't stop. The snowy cold of the water had the power to take her breath away. Cold on her knees and thighs, genitals and stomach, cold surrounding her lungs like a squeezing hand. She submerged herself, caught her breath and swam.

In high school she'd been on the swim team. Meets in the early morning. The dolphin ease of it. The endorphin rush of near-exhaustion. She'd never cared about winning, though up to a certain level she had, fairly easily. Her parents cheering for her every weekend. Her mother happy to drive her through predawn Connecticut streets. She'd had friends. They'd had parties. She had quit the swim team, started smoking cigarettes and pot, drinking in old quarries, her friends shifting, the adolescent hunger for danger. She thought of Amelia, who had never been a good swimmer, a child on the beach. At a lake. Her laughing face. Looking at her pruned fingers.

The mountain peaks around her were clear, and she watched the shadow creep across the landscape and edge into the water, turning it black. She climbed out of the lake and found the brightest sun to dry herself. She felt foolish, but she knelt on the rock with her clothes cushioning her knees and masturbated, working quickly as if she had to get something out of herself. Then she lay flat on the rock, the sun hitting her stomach and breasts and legs.

YEARS OF READING HAD, against reason and personal experience, led her to expect an epiphany. She had climbed the mountains, stripped naked at a mountain lake, in search of an answer, but she felt nothing. She felt a little different than she had before, perhaps, but not enlightened. Her burden was as heavy as it had been before. She recognized some of the sights she'd seen earlier, was fairly sure she was going in the right direction, back, but did not particularly care. At night, her hair still wet from swimming, she built a large fire and leaned toward it with her head on her knees, the warmth radiating against the crown of her head, moisture lifting off of her in clouds. The tightness of Amelia's t-shirt around her chest a comfort and a burden. She felt dumb. Nothing would ever be the same again.

SHE PUT THE TENT, her sleeping bag, the stove into the backpack and set the pack up on the trail where someone would find it. Then she walked unencumbered except for a single container of water she attached to her belt buckle with a carabiner. It was colder in the morning than it had been and she walked quickly to warm up, her hands in the pockets of her jeans. She recognized nothing.

THE TRAIL FLATTENED. She was in woods at the bottom of the mountains, where she'd started. She left the trail and walked, treading old leaves. She imagined Ted sitting in his chair in the living room, reading Chekhov, as if banking up his emotions, the dog by his feet. He was an old-fashioned man, a man who belonged in an earlier era. She thought of his broad, hairy chest, graying now, and how she had felt early on, her head against it. His particular animal scent. She missed his body. They had made a beautiful child together. But he had let Amelia leave that night. She wished she could believe in the afterlife, in angels. Such stupid things to believe in. Easier to believe that burning paper boats would transport your ancestors in the afterlife. Easier to believe in absolute nothing.

She wandered the woods until coming to an open field she had not passed before. Goldfinches flew from tree to tree at the edge of the forest, sharp yellow bursts. Beautiful things would always persist. Whether she noticed them or not. She was thirsty and tired. She knew she could dehydrate out here and die. She thought, for the first time since Amelia was found, about her students. They would arrive for class and leave fifteen minutes later, after she had failed to show, relieved, set free into the world. They would be overjoyed, but after the second week they would wonder and, maybe, worry. They didn't dislike her.

She turned around and reentered the woods. It was morning, then it was afternoon. She was thirsty and then she was dizzy, but the dizziness and the thirst passed, sending her on to a new plane. Subsistence level. As if her body were already shutting down, her thoughts feeding on themselves. She thought of Amelia in her casket. She pushed through the image to another image, Amelia in a nightgown, five years old, bare feet, standing on a chair helping her make blueberry pancakes. Morning sun through the window. The Squamish River and the town below them. Amelia was every age she had ever been. She would find a way to maintain these images so they wouldn't fade. A mental museum of her daughter through the ages. But she sensed they would fade, and quickly. There was no way to trap them. Only a select few would survive. Or maybe it was true that every memory we have is stored somewhere in our brains and the real issue is access. Her daughter's life in there, whole.

HER SWEATSHIRT SNAGGED on a tendril of prickers, the weed pulling then retracting, and she imagined her skin being pricked in the same way. Her skin would unravel and spool out as she walked and she would find herself, skinned, walking away from the last scrap of herself. She would walk through the other side of herself into a new life.

She imagined pulling out the hair on her head, black clumps falling behind, scattered by the wind.

She was hungry and thirsty and then forgot she was hungry or thirsty.

Evening was approaching.

She had been stupid to come here, but none of it had been driven by a decision on her part. Everything inevitable. She was just following, but following what?

Maybe she wouldn't make it through this. She wanted to believe she would see her daughter if she died. That Amelia would meet her walking the opposite direction in a tunnel with white light. That Amelia would take her hand and show her around.

Instead, there would be nothing. Animals would eat her body, vultures snaking their heads inside her ribcage, worms and maggots. No one would find her until spring. She thought it would be like sleeping under a warm blanket of heavy snow but knew it would be like nothing.

SHE SPOTTED A GLINT OF SILVER in the last light of day and walked toward the Volvo. Finding the car seemed momentous but not miraculous. She started the engine and maneuvered the car in increments until it was turned around. She drove down the logging road, meeting up with larger and larger roads until she was on the highway.

She pulled into a motel and got a room for the night. The attendant was old. The motel was old. The TV was like something out of her youth, and she knew if she turned it on and searched the dials she could find bad porn. She was tempted. She took a long shower. She slept.

CYNTHIA WOKE WONDERING how she'd slept with the light on the bedside table blazing white. There was a digital alarm clock on the bedstand like the digital clock of her adolescence. She remembered pressing the snooze button before getting up to work in the summer. The ice cream stand. Other teenagers. Laughter. The boy who'd insisted when he went out with her—date rape, not a term in circulation at the time. There was a black telephone with a gray face. On the gray face, raised buttons. Like an object out of another world. She reached across, scooted up on the bed, closed her eyes, pressed the numbers. Her heart beat like an alarm in her throat. She had not been so nervous to talk to him since the early, heady days of new love.

"Hello." Ted, breathless. He had been sleeping.

"It's me."

"Oh." A pause so long she wasn't sure whether he'd hung up on her. She wouldn't blame him. "Where are you?"

"You don't know?"

"No."

"Where are you right now?"

"In bed."

"Good," she said. She slid down onto the bed, rested her head on the pillow, curled onto her side. She could picture him in their bedroom, the sheet pulled down around his midsection. His paunchy stomach, his graying chest hair, his large reddish beard. God, she fucking loved him. She did. "I'm coming home," she said.

She waited for him to say something to ruin it, some stupid little something, but he didn't. She listened to his breathing for a long time.

Leaving Indian Summer

The lake house belonged to my mother's uncle, but he must have forgotten we were coming because Mother had to jimmy the door open when we arrived. Nothing to worry about, she told me, and, at ten years old, I had no choice but to believe her. For a few days we hunkered in the lake house, playing cards and reading, as rain pocked the water's surface. Mother spent most of her time playing solitaire and staring out the window. On the first clear, Indian summer day, she spent the entire morning sunning herself on the dock. I didn't mind. I loved to swim, loved the weightless feeling of submersion. At this point in my childhood, I liked to imagine myself swimming the English Channel, cold black chop bristling at my nostrils, my oiled arms churning. I also wanted to deep sea dive and fly jet airplanes, to become, somehow, a man of action. I could already sense those dreams crumbling, their irreality becoming ever clearer as I turned into something quite different, something for which I had no name.

For most of that morning, I treaded water inside a large inner tube, the black top becoming so sun-heated I could place my hand on it for only a matter of seconds, while Mother lay face-up on the dock in a red one-piece, the kind with no shoulder straps and pleats that accentuate the hips and bust, risqué for the time period. She lay as heavily as a dead thing. If I were to drown, I thought, with the morbidity of a ten-year-old, she wouldn't even realize it. Even if she were to realize, there was the question of whether or not she would save me. I believed that she would, but she would be none too happy about it. Her eyes hidden behind the lenses of dark sunglasses, it was impossible to tell whether she was asleep or awake. I alternated my gaze: from Mother to the bare blue sky, which, from my vantage point inside the inner tube, looked like a bright hole, then back again.

When a well-dressed man appeared from behind the empty boathouse and stepped onto the dock, his hard soles clopping across the planks, I bellied myself onto the inner tube, hot rubber scorching my abdomen, the sun already working to dry my soaked hair and burn the pale skin of my back. The man wore a clean, pressed, tan linen suit and a thin, dark tie. He was hatless but a hat brim had pressed a crease into his hair. When he stood above Mother's body, looking down at her, dark wings beat inside my stomach. I wanted to yell at the man, to tell him to leave, but the shape of a gun was articulated in his pocket so I held my breath and waited to see what would happen next. The moment felt packed with possibility, the future in danger of shattering.

"Ma'am," the man said.

"I'm awake," Mother said, lips curling into a grin, one she'd never directed toward me but which I had seen many times before. Sometimes, alone with me, Mother would laugh, smile, play games, but more often she was serious and thoughtful. Even happy, she seemed to hold back. The man and Mother conferred so quietly I could not hear them. After a while the man crouched beside her, his elbows on his knees, fingers lightly touching the planks of the dock. Although they were both grinning, I felt certain they were talking about something deadly serious, something so serious they couldn't help but grin. I assumed they were talking about me, an assumption strengthened by the fact that neither of them had looked in my direction. Attempting to inconspicuously paddle the tube closer, the weight of the rubber proved too great and I flipped ass-over into the water, the tube slapping the surface like a gunshot. I felt myself going under, diving like a seal, touching the scummy bottom of the lake with my chin, surfacing to blow water from my mouth and nose, all in one fluid motion, my young body full of physical ease.

"Stop fooling around, Cedric dear," Mother called, listlessly.

"Aw, now," the man said, turning his gray eyes on me. "The boy's just being a boy, Mrs. Donnolly. Isn't that right, boy?"

I returned the man's stare, regarding the crease in his hair and his fine, tan suit. Although I'd never seen him before, he was a familiar sort of man. I stood in the lake, feet touching bottom, something I hadn't done that entire morning. With my vivid imagination, I'd been picturing all kinds of evil beings lurking in the muck—lobster creatures with sharp claws, and slimy eels—but these phantasms were far from my mind as I looked at the man. If he had not been slightly wall-eyed, he would have been as handsome as a TV cop.

"Well, I guess that's all then," he told Mother, taking a fat black wallet from his suit pant pocket and making a show out of removing his card and handing it to Mother, who didn't look at it, just held it loosely between two fingers against her stomach. As soon as the man's clopping footfalls left the dock, she flicked the card into the lake, where, landing, it sent out faint ripples. My fingers ached to snatch the card—it was that close—but I could feel Mother watching me, appraising, as she so often was.

"Get out of there and get dressed," she told me.

"What was that all about?"

"Didn't I just tell you to get dressed?"

I lumbered out of the lake and onto the dock, more sea creature than human after so many hours submerged, dragging the tube after me. It was nearly as heavy as I, and it threatened to topple me back into the water, but I managed to corral it over one of the dock's pilings.

"Who was that?" I asked, standing above Mother, dripping lake water dangerously close to her shoulder.

"Do not start, Cedric. Get dressed." Mother was master of several tones of voice, and she used the one now that cut through you, a tone that said *enough* and *stop* even when you didn't know you had started anything. You had no choice but to listen.

Inside the lake house, which I had come to love—its dark wood, its ramshackle construction, its hominess—I showered and dressed in a striped t-shirt and slacks. This was the first place that had felt anything like home since we'd left Long Island. Already, that life seemed like someone else's. Life with Father. As I showered and dressed, I thought of him, and of the old house we left behind. It was small, containing nothing but the absolute essentials—two bedrooms, one bathroom, a kitchen and living space—but the ocean had been nearby. Father would enter my dark room late at night, smelling of booze and smoke, and we would both listen.

"Nothing is as big as that, Cedric," Father would say. Having grown up in Nebraska, a farm boy, the ocean was ever-new to him.

Men would often visit the house in Long Island, groups of men wearing nice suits, ties and hats, all with something slightly off about them—like the man at the dock and his wall eyes. They would talk late into the night. No matter how hard I listened, the words drifting down the hall failed to cohere. I was no longer that boy listening to the words of his father, but I was not sure who I had become yet. Reluctant to leave the lake house, I dawdled for as long as I thought I could get away with it, touching the lamp made from seashells and the rough wool of the couch.

Outside, on the drive, Mother stood waiting beside the pale blue Chevy. She'd thrown a white shirt and a black skirt on over her bathing suit, and she wore her black high heeled shoes, which made me nervous. Whenever Mother had left me alone in the house in Long Island, I would run to her bedroom, open her closet and take down the box. Hidden inside a black velvet drawstring bag within the box, the shoes had seemed like magical objects, stowed carefully. I loved to hold them in my hands. I would also try them on, but my feet were too small and I felt ridiculous shuffling along in them. Since leaving Long Island, I'd been going through a growth spurt, my bones aching painfully at night, and a secret part of me looked forward to trying the shoes on again. They fascinated me, the smooth, severe arch of the insole, the sharp wedge of the heel, the sheen of the black material. I sensed that this was an unholy attraction—my first—and that neither Father nor Mother would approve.

"Where are we going?" I asked.

"Just get in the car," she answered.

It was hard to believe Mother could see anything through the black sunglasses, but she didn't seem to have any problem. She smoked a long pink cigarette, the open windows of the Chevy letting in the Indian summer air, the local pop station playing on the radio. The Shirelles, "Baby, It's You." Sweet harmonized vocals.

The road ringing the lake was narrow and winding, and whenever we passed a car going the other way, they had to slow down and steer to the side, sometimes onto someone's scruffy lawn; Mother certainly wasn't moving aside. She simply kept driving, elbow out the window, acrid smoke from her cigarette blowing across my face as if by divine intervention, no matter the wind direction.

She parked at Nero's, a fried seafood and burger joint overlooking the lake at the end of the road, where we'd bought many of our meals already. Since it was offseason, the red shack was dead, and I ordered from a tired-looking woman with greasy brown hair who wanted nothing more than to close for the winter. I ate sitting next to Mother in the car, careful to keep the ketchup drips on the wax paper and off my slacks.

"Aren't you hungry?" I asked.

"No. No, I'm not. But thank you for thinking about me. That's sweet. You're a sweet boy." Her tone of voice was different now, a tone that came from some small part of her and wavered out into space.

"Are they going to take me away from you?" I asked between bites of burger.

"Who? The guy with the eyes? Did you see his eyes, Cedric? At first you think he's perfectly normal, and then you take a second look and it's, oh boy. He was a funny fellow, wasn't he? Nobody's going to take you away from me, Cedric. Nobody. Ever." The hamburger tasted faintly of fish, faintly of coconut because of the smell of Mother's skin, faintly of smoke. "Eat up now," she said. She stared at the lake, and I wondered what she was seeing. I had the sense that she was thinking about Father, but that was a subject I didn't dare broach.

The lake wasn't large, but, because the sun was out for the first time in a long time and because it was early fall with a few trees starting to yellow and redden, it was beautiful. Wondering why this time of year was called Indian summer, I pictured Indians sprinting like ghosts between the trees, wearing almost nothing, their faces marked with red and black smudges. There was an unknown world just behind the visible one, and all I needed to do was look harder and I would see something fantastic.

After I tossed the wax paper and Styrofoam drink container into a red wire trash barrel, mother backed out of Nero's and sped toward the modest main street of town, a place that had not changed in a hundred years. When we first drove into town, the rain had made everything resemble a gloomy postcard, but now the white clapboards of the bank and the general store and the handful of tourist shops looked pristine in the sunlight. A black clock tower showed us the time: 3:10. It was a town that tugged at the simplest desires of my ten-year-old soul—home, stability, tradition. I yearned without knowing what I yearned for or how to couch it in language.

After angling the Chevy into a narrow space in front of the bank, Mother swiveled her head, taking in both sides of the sidewalk.

"You'd better come in," she said, grabbing her purse, her tone changed once again, to one I'd never heard before. It was harried.

The interior of the bank was quiet, solemn, and clean, reminding me of a library or a church, two places that seemed exotic to me, maybe because I had not spent much time in either one. It smelled of recently cleaned carpet. Mother directed me to a leather chair by the front door then conferred with a banker with a thin mustache and thinner hair, who could not stop smiling at her. He held a gate open for her then led her to a small room near the vault. Mother held a small key in her hand, the white and black of her clothes setting off a nice contrast. Her hair was black, her skin white. A striking woman.

As I waited, I imagined what it would feel like to be a bank robber. It seemed as if it would be fairly easy to barge in with a pistol, a bandana covering my mouth, demanding the mealy-faced tellers empty their drawers into a burlap sack. I didn't see anything that could prevent it. I imagined the surge of energy that would come from holding such power. It was a pleasant thing to think about as the sun streamed in, finding me in the leather chair, muscles sore from the morning's long swim.

When she emerged from the room beside the vault, Mother's purse bulged and she walked with a clipped gait. I barely had time to follow her out the door and hop into the car before she was reversing onto the road in a wide arc, then jamming the gearshift forward, the car jumping onto the pavement. When she passed the road that would have taken us back to the lake house, I closed my eyes and breathed slowly.

"Where are we going?" It occurred to me that, unlike Mother, I had only one tone of voice.

"I don't know yet. I've always wanted to see California, but that's stupid. I know that's stupid. Canada is just a few hours away. We could be there by morning."

"Canada?"

"I know, I know. But there are cities there, too, Cedric. Toronto, maybe. I don't know. Don't ask questions."

Before we had arrived at the lake house and Mother had jimmied the door open, we'd driven from state to state, New York, Connecticut, Massachusetts, staying for a few days at a time with old friends of Mother's, mostly women with shorter hair and longer dresses than my mother, and husbands. They smiled kindly at me, but it seemed to take an effort. Some could hardly look away from their infant children. They lived in large homes full of fine furniture, the fathers in rumpled suits returning from long days at the office and going straight for the liquor cabinet. The men would look at me with odd expressions—expressions of regret and approbation and warning and, worst of all, pity. We would stay at one home for a few days, then move on to the next. Since Father had disappeared, everything felt temporary.

"Probably dead," I heard Mother say again. This was her answer any time I asked about him. I didn't believe her. He seemed so real to me—not a substantial man, maybe, but real. His blond hair darkened with brilliantine, his wrists showing above the cuffs of his suit jacket when he leaned forward. I could smell the booze and cigarette odors that wafted off of him in my bedroom. The endless ocean.

Once, he took me to the beach long after dark, and under a huge moon we shot at gulls with a small pistol. We hadn't intended to actually kill anything, but Father clipped one on the wing and it walked in a funny circle, squawking.

"Jesus Christ," he said. "Would you look at that? I shot it." He seemed unable to believe what had just happened had happened. He shot it in the head to put it out of its misery.

"I left all my clothes at the lake house," I told Mother. "I was reading a book."

"I brought your clothes." She gestured to the back, where she had shoved her bag. "And we can always buy you a new book. They have books in Canada, too, Cedric. Where's your spirit of adventure?"

"I should be in school right now," I said.

"Oh, shut up, Cedric. Most kids would love to be out of school. Most kids would *exult*." I didn't know what that word meant, but it sounded ominous and final.

We drove north for a few hours, and for a few hours I tried to sulk, but sulking is pointless if people insist on ignoring you. Mother was clearly not thinking about me, about my childish fears and concerns. She smoked one cigarette after another and tried to keep a pop station tuned in on the radio. When we got farther north, we were out of range and all there was was silence in the car. The mountains loomed larger. The day was cloud-free, the sun fierce and beautiful, the trees taking on more and more colors. After a while, I couldn't help but feel okay.

It was almost evening when we pulled into a scenic turnoff on a mountain highway. The sky was stitched-together ribbons of color—pinks and oranges, mostly. Mother turned off the engine, got out and stood before a drop-off, while I sat in the car watching her. She was the most beautiful woman I had ever seen. In a way that I would not understand until much later, and then only imperfectly, I wanted to *be* her. I wanted to wear her black skirt, her white shirt and high heels, and I wanted to stand before a mountain cliff looking at the sunset, absolutely ignorant of what the future held.

Mother did a strange thing then. Unhurried, and as if it were the most natural thing in the world, she stepped out of her skirt and her white shirt, and she removed her red one-piece, pealing it from her body as if it were a second skin. She stood naked for a matter of seconds, though it felt much longer, facing the sun. The day's sunbathing had bronzed parts of her, while other parts remained pale white. A patchwork woman. She stepped back into the skirt and buttoned the shirt, then bunched the swimsuit in her hand and dropped it onto a boulder, where it resembled nothing so much as a pool of blood.

Back in the car, sans sunglasses now, her eyes were encased in lines, but sharp, as if everything had become focused within her. It seemed as if she could see through things, as if something in her asserted womanhood had given her new powers.

"No more moping for me, Cedric," she said. "I just shook myself out of it. I'm ready to go get 'em."

"That was disgusting."

"Well, you didn't have to watch, now, did you? And you don't want me to sit here in an uncomfortable bathing suit all night, do you? Is that what you want?" She pulled the Chevy back onto the mountain road. "Everyone's naked under their clothes, Cedric. Even fat people."

It was supposed to be a joke, so I smiled, but Mother didn't bother to look over to catch it.

At the next general store we bought a few days' supply of junk food: beef jerky, cupcakes, fruit pies, chips, and sodas, and while we drove even farther north we munched on food and sang a few songs. Ninety-nine bottles of beer on the wall, and over the river and through the woods. It was possible, momentarily, to believe that we, just the two of us, constituted a normal family. But Father was always on the edge of my thoughts, intruding.

When full night arrived, the atmosphere inside the car changed, becoming solemn. I was tired and yearned for sleep, but no matter how hard I tried I couldn't fall asleep. A few stars broke through the black mat of night like bad magic. Everyone *knows* the dove will disappear.

"Your father never would have gotten anywhere without me." Mother spoke into the darkness, as if continuing a discussion we'd never started. I was going to remind her that he was "probably dead," but I didn't. "He owes it all to me. Big man? I don't think so. He came from Nebraska, for God's sake. He didn't know his ass from his elbow, Cedric, until I pointed it out to him. This here's your ass, I told him, this here's your elbow, now go on and do something, for God's sake. I introduced him to people. Do you think we would have had that house in Long Island if I had left it up to him? He would have been happy as a soda jerk or a milkman. Sometimes you have to force people to rise to their own possibilities." She grew quiet and taut, her lighter throwing her face into stark white relief.

"What happened to him? Really?"

"You're too young to know yet."

"What do you mean? Why?"

"Your father got into trouble, that's all. He did things he didn't want to do. He listened to the wrong people. It was just a mistake. He was sorry to leave you, though, I can tell you that. You stick with me and you'll be a stronger man than *he* ever was."

I would not unbury my father until years later, when what my mother had done—to him, and to a number of other men before him—became clear. At that moment, in the car, speeding through the mountains into the coming night, I believed every word she said, and it was enough to sustain me. My father had been sorry to leave me. Maybe he was not dead after all. Maybe he would find us in Canada. I pictured him knocking on the door to an apartment, waiting for us, for *me*, to answer. I couldn't picture the city or Canada clearly, but I could picture him rapping on the door until his knuckles bled.

It was full dark and all of the stars were out when we pulled next to three vehicles before a crude campsite. We couldn't have been far from the Canadian border by that point. Two of the vehicles were Chevys, like ours only newer, while the third was a Cadillac.

"That's more like it. All it takes is a little faith. Leave the talking to me, Cedric."

I followed her. The air was colder than it had been during the day, turning my skin to gooseflesh. We walked into the dark woods in the direction of a campfire flickering not far from the road. I was surprised Mother could walk through the woods in her high heels, but she managed. It was a large fire, with logs the size of small trees burning in its center. The laughter of men sounded like the barking of dogs.

"Look at that," Mother said, pointing to a deer carcass hanging from the crux of a tree, the innards pooled beneath it, alive with flies. "Barbarians," she said, though not in a disapproving tone. The meat glistened with reflected firelight, and the deer's eyes glittered. We moved deeper into the woods, closer to the fire.

"Are you boys trying to attract bears?" Mother said when she stepped into the circle of firelight. Four men turned to look at her, their faces frozen in mid-laughter, unable at first to comprehend what had just emerged from the woods— Woman. Sizing them up quickly, Mother walked to the most clean-cut among them, a man with a day's worth of stubble, black hair pomaded straight back, and an unrumpled flannel shirt, and settled onto the log beside him. The other three men were lumpy, one wearing a beard, the other two too common to differentiate. Four tents were arranged in a semi-circle behind the fire. Mother pressed her legs close together, pulled the skirt over her knees, reached her hands out toward the flames, and grinned at them. "That deer is awfully close to your campsite."

"We got all the meat we want," one of the men said. "The bears can have what's left."

"We got the fire and we got guns. We're not afraid of bears," the bearded man said.

"It still seems foolish to hang a carcass right *there*... But what do I know? Do any of you have an extra tent for me and my boy? We got off course and need a place to sleep for the night. We're traveling up to Canada."

"Plenty of room in my tent."

"Howard," the clean-cut man reproached, speaking for the first time. "Maybe you've never seen one, but this here is a lady. I'll bunk with the animal here, and you and your boy can have my tent. Come on, boy, have a seat." I'd been standing, half believing and half wishing I was invisible. I wanted to leave but couldn't.

"Thank you," Mother said. "That's kind of you."

"Could I offer you a drink?" The man lifted a bottle from behind the log, brown liquid shining in firelight, and raised his eyebrows.

"I'd like that," Mother said. She upended the bottle, and the men and I watched her throat muscles move. After five or six seconds, they were cheering for her. "Would you look at that?" one of them said. She wiped her mouth on the sleeve of her white shirt and passed the bottle to the man on the next log.

"It's a fine night," Mother said. "Isn't it?"

Something had changed around the fire. The men had been nothing but men before—drunk, laughing, out hunting and ducking out on their wives—but now they weren't sure what they were anymore. I crossed before the fire, lay my head in Mother's lap, and listened to them talk while

Mother ran her fingers through my hair. From their conversation, I gathered they were professional men up from Boston, that the clean-cut man was a lawyer. The rhythm of their conversation and the warmth of the fire lulled me, and even though I was suspicious of the men and afraid of what might happen next, before long I drifted asleep.

When I awoke, the lawyer's face was inches from mine, so close liquor fumes cleared my sinuses.

"Hey kid," he whispered. "Your mother and I are going into my tent to talk a little bit. I want you to take this, and if anyone comes near the tent I want you to fire it into the air. You got it?" He pressed a rifle into my stomach and giggled. It was disconcerting to hear a grown man giggle—a new thing in the world. The fire had burned down to glowing coals. Turning, I caught sight of Mother's legs, Mother's high heels disappearing behind the flap of a canvas tent. I sat up, tried to gain some sense of clarity.

"Do you understand what I'm saying?" the lawyer said. "I'm counting on you, son." He could barely stop himself from laughing. I nodded, holding the rifle awkwardly across my chest. The rifle felt small, the wood stock smooth in my hands. "There's a good boy," he said.

After the man followed my mother into the tent, I stood, so exhausted I could barely control my body. My legs carried me closer to the tent, then toward the fire. Finally I steadied myself and stood in the darkness, ramrod straight. I imagined I was a soldier in the war and Japs were invading the island. Father had been in Guam during the war. He'd once told me about running up a hill in a jungle while people shot at him—how amazed he'd been to survive, to make it to the top of that hill, only to realize that there were other hills after that. Hill after hill after hill. I could almost hear Father's voice coming out of the darkness. What remained of the fire sounded like the ocean. I wished I was back in Long

Island, that he was in the bedroom with me, that nothing had changed.

The night was so dark—clouds having covered the moon—it was almost liquid. I remembered tipping over into the lake that morning, how I'd felt like a seal swimming through the water. I realized then, for the first time, that I didn't want to be a soldier or a jet pilot or a deep-sea diver. I wanted to be a seal. I wanted to be Mother. I wanted to be liquid. I wanted to throw the rifle far away from me, but I had been given orders. I tried to get back into the fantasy.

There were Japs all over the island, sneaking out from behind the trees. Japs and Indians, hunting me down. I held the rifle to my shoulder, sighted down the barrel, tried to ignore the sounds coming from the tent. The red coals flared and brought shapes to life around me. Any one of them could have been an enemy soldier.

When a figure did lumber toward me, I simply reacted. I flicked the safety off—my father had taught me to do that, on the beach, years before—and pressed the trigger, absorbing the kickback. The flare of the barrel illuminated the surprised face of the bearded hunter.

"Ah fuck," he shouted. "You fucking shot me, you little shit." The hunter went down. Commotion followed. Behind me, the lawyer emerged from the tent, hurrying toward his friend, and my mother grabbed me by the arm. She whispered "hold these," handing me her shoes, and we ran through the woods toward the car. The air was saturated black, and branches brushed our faces and arms, but we didn't pause until we were inside the car and Mother was starting the engine, turning around and speeding forward with a shriek of rubber, the mountain road and the surrounding woods washed yellow in our headlights.

I held the shoes in my lap, absently fingering the smooth arches, wondering why I didn't feel ashamed or worried, fearful or confused. I didn't understand the concept of shock at that age—I was simply grateful to be removed from those anticipated feelings. I had just shot a man. In the darkness under the seat, where Mother couldn't see, I removed my sneakers and put the high heeled shoes on my bare feet. The warmth of my mother's feet ghosted inside. The shoes were still slightly too large for me, but someday, I knew, they would fit perfectly.

Mother buttoned her white shirt and laughed.

"You did good," she said. "Don't you worry about anything. You did good, Cedric. Look at this." She threw a leather wallet into my lap. When I opened it, a fan of large bills unfurled. "I can't stand lawyers," she said.

While she drove those mountain roads, I had a hard time picturing anything. My future had been ripped open and rearranged, and suddenly that seemed like a good thing. I liked the smooth feel of the high heels' insoles against my bare feet and the cash in my lap. I liked the fact that everything was unknown and open, and that we were finally together in something, Mother and I.

Mousekiller

Santamaria first noticed the decapitated mouse beside the drain five minutes into his shower, which meant he'd been standing with his bare feet no more than a couple inches from the dead, soggy body for five minutes. Because the drain was partially clogged with hair from his wife and daughter, the rinse water had backed up, and bacteria and germs from the dead mouse had probably already touched his bare feet. Crouching to inspect the corpse, Santamaria was suddenly aware of his nudity, his balls dangling to touch the smooth white shell of the tub, water running over the knobs of his spine and into his buttcrack. In place of the mouse's head was a red, mangled knot of flesh. Squeamishly, Santamaria lowered a dark blue washcloth over the body, feeling tiny ribs and ill-defined muscles through the nap of the material. He placed it, like a nice little package, on the side of the tub, turned the shower knob to the left for hotter water and, in the ensuing steam, vigorously scrubbed his hands and feet.

After the shower, he dressed in gray sweatpants and a Henley then ambled downstairs. His wife, Leidy, sat in the kitchen wearing a thin nightgown and patting the cat, who perched on top of the table purring and rubbing his body against Leidy's hand. The nightgown was open, displaying two long breasts tipped with nipples the size and shape of pencil erasers. Santamaria took note of the breasts, made himself a cup of coffee. Chock Ful O' Nuts. He missed the good stuff, but they had cut their expenses to the bone. No more going out to eat, no more Netflix, no more cable or cable internet. He was grateful he'd been able to talk Leidy out of selling his iPhone on eBay—how was he going to take calls from prospective employers if he didn't have a cell phone?

Santamaria settled down at the table to eat his daily dose of Raisin Bran and drink his coffee, and they both listened to Ramona, their daughter, slam her bedroom door upstairs, then slam the bathroom door. She was eleven going on sixteen. Ramona had started menstruating when she was ten and a half, and ever since then it had been watch out. Childhood was already a distant memory, for all of them. It had been bad enough when Santamaria had seen Ramona talking with older boys on the way home from the bus stop, laughing too loudly, but when he caught her smoking with one of them in the turnaround at the end of the road it had taken all he had in him not to hit her. They were losing her— he was sure of it. Staying home didn't seem to be helping matters the way he'd hoped it would. A person could get consumed with worry.

The cat was now perched on Leidy's lap, staring at him, Sphinxlike, with two yellow eyes.

"Cover yourself up, will you."

"There's nothing here you haven't seen already," she said, opening the nightgown a little wider. "Besides, I thought you *liked* these."

"Please, Leidy."

Santamaria had met his wife at his place of employment thirteen years earlier. She'd packed boxes in the shipping department while he'd worked in the art department as a production artist. The difference in their stations had given him the upper hand for a little while, but not for long. Leidy was forty-two now, but looked thirty, tops. He, on the other hand, was forty-five but looked fifty. If either of them was going to have an affair, it was pretty clear which one it would be. Forty-five years old, but still, like a school kid, the sight of his wife's familiar breasts gave Santamaria an uncontrollable erection. She shot him a sly, sexy smile just before Ramona screamed in the bathroom. It was a no-shit, full throttle scream, sending Santamaria's paternal feelings into automatic pilot. His daughter was in danger—he had to help her. He shot up, adrenaline giving him the strength of three men, then sat back down.

"There's a dead mouse in the bathroom," he said.

"There's a what?"

"There's a dead mouse in the bathroom. Your little champion there ripped its head off. I'll take care of it once Mona's done."

"Isn't he a good little mousekiller," Leidy said, her tone of voice changing mid-sentence, becoming higher and sweeter as she shifted her attention, from Santamaria to the cat.

AFTER THE TWO WOMEN in his life had left—their hair combed, eyes shadowed, skin moisturized, etc., etc.—Santamaria removed the blue washcloth from the bathroom and carried it downstairs, gingerly. He was not a man who did many things gingerly, but mice tweaked him. He carried the washcloth outside, the mouse body disgustingly perceptible beneath the terrycloth. Bile built in the back of Santamaria's throat, but his curiosity got the better of him, and inside the shed he placed the package on his workbench and unpeeled the folds of washcloth. The fluorescent tubes flickered, Frankensteinishly. He imagined a reanimated mouse wreaking havoc on the neighborhood. The longer he was out of work, he noticed, the more often asinine fantasies played themselves out in his head. Soon he would lose all ability to communicate with other adults. He imagined the headless mouse scratching blindly at foundations. Realistically, there was not all that much it could do if it did come back to life.

The mouse's fur was gray and black, moist from the shower, the skin of the body paler, pinker. Where the head had been was a raw fold of mouse body material. Santamaria pressed the mouse's belly with his finger, then held the finger away from him. He imagined the crunch of separating bones. He laid the carcass on some window mesh left over from when he'd replaced the window screens, then buried the mouse in the yard, about six inches deep. In a few weeks he'd lift the mesh up and all that would remain of the mouse would be a skeleton, sans skull. He had learned this valuable skill in Boy Scouts. His childhood bedroom had been decorated with lizard skulls and snake skeletons and the skeletons of raccoons he found on the road, dead but not yet squished beyond all recognition. Back then he'd been less squeamish, though even as a child mice had creeped him out.

At ten o'clock he went upstairs to the master bedroom, moved the cat out of the sunbeam that fell across the bed, and stretched out on the covers. The house had been a ranch when they'd moved in, but in the mid-nineties Santamaria had made a bundle in the stocks and they'd refi-ed and had the addition built. Two bedrooms and a bathroom. Their master bedroom let in light throughout the day—a fact he hadn't been aware of until last year when he'd been laid off. He curled into a ball and fell asleep.

Fifteen minutes later he was awakened by the sound of shrieking—distinctly miniature shrieking—followed by the clatter of the cat bumping into things in hot pursuit around the bed. Although he felt exposed lying there in the sunbeam, as if the mouse was going to run up the bed and over his face, he didn't move, merely watched the hunt. The cat was Genghis Khan-cruel, biting and releasing, pouncing, placing the limp mouse in its mouth and sinking its needle-like teeth into the shrieking body. So, an infestation. One mouse could be just one mouse, but two mice meant a shitload of other mice.

TEN MINUTES LATER, Santamaria pulled his white Alero into the parking lot of the hardware store, almost empty at this time of morning. He'd bought the Alero, a mid-level sports car, for Leidy, but she'd never grown comfortable with the stick shift, so every day she drove his Grand Am to Atlantic City, where she worked as a cocktail waitress in one of the casinos, wearing not nearly enough clothes. That job would not last forever—because, no matter how good she looked now, forty-two was still forty-two.

Behind the counter of the hardware store, Bob Woodward hunched. Woodward and Santamaria had conjoined backyards, but a barrier of overgrown shrubs meant they hardly ever saw each other. Woodward was the same age as Santamaria—maybe a little older. It was the Great Recession, and you were lucky if you had a job, but it was hard not to feel bad for Bob. His eyes shifted downward.

"Morning, Bob. You having mice problems over at your place?"

"Nope," Woodward said. "You?"

"I'm afraid so. You think I should poison the suckers or go old school with the traps?"

"The traps don't always kill 'em. Sometimes you have to finish the job yourself. But on the other hand when you poison 'em they find some cozy out-of-the-way place to rot and stink your house up. There's those so-called 'humane' traps that can trap any number of them, just bait it with peanut butter, but you have to be sure to empty those real quick because I've seen it that one of them will eat the others, and then it's a hell of a mess to clean up."

"Right," Santamaria said. He pictured hordes of headless mice devouring each other. The image was imprecise—how the hell would they eat each other without heads?—but no less disturbing for that.

"So, how's the job search going?" Woodward asked as Santamaria carried an armload of wooden traps with metal snaps to the register. He figured seven would do. He hoped so.

"Same old same old. You hiring here?"

"I'm afraid not, Bill." At one time, not so long ago, they would have been joking, ribbing each other.

After the hardware store, Santamaria drove fast down the long straight roads of rural, South Jersey, a town called Buena, pronounced Bue-nah not Bway-nah, although Mexicans had staked a pretty large section of town now. The fields were dying or dead, plowed over or under, the trees had lost all of their leaves, and the sky had the bleached look it would keep until spring returned. Santamaria hated to think about the prospect of another winter at home, unemployed. When he saw a small wake of vultures hopping around near the roadside, he pictured millions of them darkening the skies, plucking at his eyeballs and ribcage. I'm still alive, guys, he imagined screaming, but they didn't pay any attention to him.

NOW THERE WERE THREE MICE in the bedroom, and the cat looked dizzy and tired. He was an adept hunter, a skilled mousekiller, but he had his paws full. Santamaria cheered him on, surprised by his own voice. "Get 'em, boy. Come on and get 'em." The cat didn't even look at him. He had turned completely feral now. You can tame a dog or a bird, but you cannot tame a cat.

As he made lunch downstairs—a grilled cheese sandwich, the cheese bright orange because he'd bought the wrong kind at Shoprite—he listened to the skittering and crashing of the cat upstairs. Every sound sent ripples of disgust through him. Eating, he tried not to think about hairy, diseased mice or their headless carcasses, but his mind had a mind of its own. He imagined hundreds of the little bastards scurrying over the bed while he and Leidy tried to sleep. He imagined them in Ramona's hair and coming out of Leidy's mouth. Somehow he was able to finish the sandwich. He read the sports page and the comics and then skimmed the front page.

Since the cat was still working in the bedroom, Santamaria took his iPhone into the bathroom to masturbate to internet porn, hooking into his neighbor's Wi-Fi. This was about the only thing he did with the iPhone anymore—he wasn't about to check the few stocks he still owned and see that the absolute bottom was even lower than expected—and he'd become adept with manipulating the thing with his left hand while manipulating himself with the right. Afterwards he was filled with overwhelming sadness, remorse, and self-disgust, but then he flushed the soiled Kleenex and washed his hands and had nothing else to do for the day.

There were four, possibly five mice in the bedroom now. They scattered when he came near. He baited the traps with orange cheese, laid them around the edge of the bedroom and waited.

Sitting on the couch in the living room, he looked at the front yard. After a while the cat came down and stared at him, as if the traps had absolved him of his responsibilities. The cat was mostly black with little bits of white on its chest and paws. He was Leidy's cat, but, since Santamaria had been laid off, they had developed a relationship. Once in a while the cat let him pat it, or curled up on his lap, a warm bundle at his crotch, but now the cat just stared at Santamaria. He imagined it was sucking out his soul, like some kind of feline witch. If you thought about them in a certain way, cats were the spookiest thing in the world. Upstairs, it sounded like a mouse convention was underway. They were partying, wearing little hats, falling into the punch bowl. He waited for the snap of a trap, but, even after half an hour, it had not come.

IT WAS AMAZING HOW MANY PEOPLE frequented a casino at two o'clock in the afternoon. They looked like they didn't know whether it was day or night, and didn't care. Some of them looked like they hadn't left the casino for weeks. They had the worn-away appearance of refugees.

Santamaria sat at one of the old-fashioned slot machines watching Leidy from a distance. She wore a gold miniskirt, her strong, long legs on full display, stiletto heels, a gold lamé top that dipped in the front and back. Sometimes after she came home, he would rub her feet for her. Heels were like medieval torture devices, she told him, but they were sexy as hell. Some of the men at the slots were watching her, too, but she was just one of several waitresses exposing too much of their bodies. Santamaria was jealous and proud and turned on and pissed off. She made more as a cocktail waitress than he'd ever made at any of his jobs. He'd worked his way up from file boy to production artist to middle manager before getting canned. He didn't have any skills to speak of—beyond Excel and PowerPoint and a little Adobe Illustrator. He had mostly scheduled work for the art department, a glorified secretary.

He fed his credit card into the machine and began playing—what the hell, why not. Maybe he'd win twenty thousand and they could pay off their credit card debt. The machine still had an arm, but it had been retrofitted with buttons. He couldn't stand the newer machines with their cartoon interfaces. He preferred big red, white, and blue 7s and cherries, rollers that actually rolled.

"Can I get you a drink, sir," Leidy asked, her slightly husky voice—she'd smoked for almost twenty years before he'd finally convinced her to quit—flirtatious but changing quickly when he turned around and she recognized him. "What are *you* doing here?" she said, her voice taking on the accent it always did when she was angry. His Colombian princess. Avenging angel. Her hand went automatically to her hip.

"Calm down," he said. "I figured I'd apply at the casinos. There's nothing else around."

"You apply online, dummy. No wonder you can't get a job."

"You know I'm trying."

"And what are you doing playing the slots, moron? You know you can't win, right?"

He hit the button and won twenty dollars, electronic blips tallying his credits, looked at her and grinned.

"Go," she said. "Just go." He watched her walk away, her hips swaying. Her ass was almost nothing at all now. She worked out too much, didn't eat enough. There was something both sexual and asexual about her body. Why couldn't he have married a schoolteacher or something? What was she going to do in a few years when no one wanted to look at all that skin except for him? What were *they* going to do?

THE ATLANTIC CITY LIBRARY was packed with people, many of whom did not speak English. A number of locals were at the computer kiosks. English tutoring sessions were in progress at many of the tables. It was the most crowded and claustrophobia-inducing library Santamaria had ever seen, like the casinos without the electronic jangling or the delusion of winning. He put his name on a long list of people waiting to use the computers, found a magazine, and waited to grab one of the chairs in the magazine and newspapers room. Finally an old woman wearing a white winter hat collected her plastic bags and left. Her odor—a kind of vegetable rot—permeated the chair, and he imagined thousands of tiny microbes invading all of his pores. Still, the chair was comfortable and he became accustomed to the smell quickly enough.

These are your people now, Santamaria told himself, looking at the locals. He didn't want to look down on them, but part of him did. He'd been raised in a suburb of Philadelphia. His family had never had a lot of money, but they had always had some. He had been strictly middle class—Italian but not Italian Italian. He'd gotten the job at the merchandising company, worked his way up. Everything had seemed easy and inevitable. His middle manager wages allowed him to play with stocks, and he had hit on some, big time. Then everything had crashed, he lost a bundle, and here he was. The heady scent of body odor escaped from the sleeping man beside him. A Chinese grandmother stared at him from across the room, probably waiting for the chair. His skin crawled. He imagined that the five mice had turned into a hundred, two hundred, five hundred, back at their house. He imagined five hundred mouse heads lined up on the stairs, staring at him. He wondered where that first mouse head had gone. Did the cat *eat* it?

Finally, he got his half an hour on the computer—time enough to fill out one application for Caesar's. The application process included a lengthy questionnaire that asked questions about what he would do in certain situations and which of two things—honesty or reliability, say—was more important, a questionnaire about his values. He felt violated but answered the questions the way he imagined they wanted him to answer them, without attending to his actual beliefs.

BACK AT THE HOUSE, Ramona shot him a look of pure hatred. She sat at the kitchen table, a shoebox in front of her.

"Hey, bud," he said. "How was school?" He had never needed to take a shower as desperately as he did now.

"Mousekiller," she said.

"Huh?"

"This was the only one that was still alive," she gestured at the box, opened it. Inside, a small gray mouse limped around. *Vermin* was the word that came to mind. "I already buried the other ones in the backyard. How *could* you?"

He shrugged, feeling monstrous.

"We should really put him out of his misery, Mona," he said. Ramona pushed a piece of wilted lettuce against the injured mouse's face. It seemed to look up at them in anguish.

"I'm going to nurse him back to health."

"Sweetie, listen. He's going to die. If not now, then soon." It felt rotten, but also kind of good, to be imparting life lessons to his daughter. It felt fatherly and grown-up. Sometimes we have to do things we don't want to do. "He's going to die real soon. Let me just put him out of his misery." He pictured himself pressing a tiny pillow against the mouse's face, holding the pillow there while the mouse struggled for breath. He pictured stabbing the mouse in the chest with a tiny dagger. He hoped Caesar's would call him. Even a shitty job as a security guard would be better than this. Anything but another long winter.

HE LISTENED HARD BUT HEARD no skittering mice that night—not that he could sleep anyway. From Ramona's room came the sound of the injured mouse struggling to escape the shoebox. He pictured the box scraping across the hardwood floors, a centimeter at a time. He was tempted to take the box and throw the mouse outside, but he knew Ramona would never forgive him. Eventually the thing would die all on its own. The cat mewled outside Ramona's room. Santamaria felt fur replacing his hair, tiny mouse teeth replacing his real teeth. He was itchy. Whenever he closed his eyes, he saw mice and tiny bacteria. He wondered how many organisms had been living on that library chair he'd sat in, how many germs were on the keyboard he'd used. Leidy had not had sex with him in three weeks, and she showed no signs of needing or wanting any ever again. Was she cheating on him? She'd seemed awfully upset when he showed up at work. He pictured her with a Mexican busboy in the employee's corridors of the casino. He would have to do something nice for her. If she hadn't cheated on him yet, she might any day. Flowers, dinner? He couldn't afford anything. Maybe he could write her a poem.

In the morning, he pretended to sleep, listening to the two women in his life get ready and leave for school and work. When he was making the bed—Leidy would be impressed—he found the mouse's head. It was a tiny, hairy ball. He picked it up with his fingers, not nearly as disgusted as he would have expected. He held the head up to the sunbeam coming through the window. The eyes of the mouse were open, staring out with animal wonder. It was the strangest thing he'd ever seen. Fascinating and frightening, a talisman from another world. He thought about running a thread through its ears and wearing it as a necklace.

The sole remaining mouse was still in the shoebox. Ramona had taped down the lid and poked holes in the top, and every once in a while the whiskers of the mouse poked out of the holes. Santamaria carried it downstairs and put the box on the kitchen table. He figured he could go back to the library once a day for the next month and still have more casinos to apply to. The cat hopped up on his lap and purred, rubbing his head up against Santamaria's hand. He had some decisions to make.

Dogs

The dogs were all the same: German Shepherds that had been made mean. The dogs had a room of their own in our father's apartment in Lowell we were not allowed to enter, not that we wanted to. When we first showed up the dogs—two, sometimes three—would bark like crazy, repetitive threats that would suddenly stop. We would forget about the dogs, but then one of us would walk past the door and from behind would come snarls, guttural sounds that raised the hackles on our necks. When we slept, in one room we were sure was smaller than the dogs' room, a glorified laundry closet with three cots covered with slick nylon sleeping bags, red, green, and navy blue, we imagined the dogs being let loose from their room, their nails clattering on the linoleum floors. We imagined them finding us, lunging, their teeth at our tender necks. We imagined bleeding out and screaming, our father watching from the doorway with a sad expression on his face, not sure which to save: his kid or his dog.

We would see them from the back window of the bathroom whenever he let them out. They were painfully beautiful: sleek brown and black dogs with perfect triangular ears. Sometimes they would wrestle each other, nipping and growling, and we would recognize something inside ourselves.

I hate those fucking dogs, Steven said.

Our father ate pizza, microwave meals, canned soups. He never cooked anything. He smelled like cigarette smoke and leather and dogs and sex. We didn't know that was the smell then, but something inside us recognized it. There was always a woman around the apartment. She would either ignore us or try to play games with us—games that were usually too young for us. War and Connect Four. We wanted to feed her to the dogs, watch her get her limbs pulled off, imagined the dogs sinking their teeth into that soft, tender spot on her white neck we saw pulsating. She was always skinny and pale, usually blonde, sometimes with bad blue tattoos. They would watch movies on the couch together.

Once we were there when one of the dogs got loose and someone showed up at the door with their son all bloody and said, your dog did this. Your fucking dog, Palonco. You're gonna pay for this. Yeah yeah, our father said. He put on his leather jacket and told us to follow him. He carried the leash lashed around his hand. It was dark and cold and we didn't know these streets at all. There were alleys and people on stoops and he called his dog—Sarge—and whistled, and we followed behind him sure that the dog was going to find us first. The boy at the apartment had been covered in blood, parts of his skin hanging loose. His eyes had been watery but he hadn't been crying. He'd stared straight ahead like there was nothing inside. We didn't know where the boy had come from, and we never saw him again.

I should shoot that fucking dog, our father said, but we knew he wouldn't. When we found the dog near a small park it cowered, a smattering of blood around its muzzle. Our father yelled at it, but we could tell he was proud, that he wanted the dog to get loose and bite a thousand more little boys, wanted it to gnaw at ears and legs, wanted it to strike fear in the hearts of all the residents of the small mill city. He wanted a dog of raw meat and muscle, a dog of jaw and fang and claw. His forearms were taut as he reined in the beast.

Later that night we heard him go into the room where the dogs stayed. We heard the door close quietly, latching behind him. We listened and we wondered what he was doing in there, wondered how he gave love to his wanted things.

Lost Mothers

My son returned a month after the funeral. He was sleeping sweetly in his bed. I wanted to wake him right away. I wanted to shake him gently and hold him against my body, tell him how much I had missed him and loved him. But I didn't dare. What if he were actually dead, again? What if he vanished the second I touched him? I sat on the edge of his bed and looked at the crown of his head, where his hair swirled, at the backs of his stick-out ears, at the nape of his neck. The covers rose and fell; he was breathing.

I felt an overwhelming tenderness for this boy's body. I had mourned so intensely the past month had felt like three years. Mourning had trained me to be circumspect about miracles. I sat on the edge of his bed, a simple black frame to which he had affixed stickers of cartoon characters, without taking my eyes off him, the morning out the window at first gray then green and finally almost white in its intensity.

I wanted to call somebody—Stephan, my mother, my old friend Jenn, one of my new acquaintances from the support group—but how could I share this news with anyone? I was either insane or the world was not what we had thought it was. When Stephan returned from Barcelona, a conference he could not miss, he would help me decide how to accommodate this new Wyatt into our lives. Until then I had Wyatt to myself, so there were no decisions to be made.

The longer he slept the more I worried that he had not returned at all, that I was seeing an earlier version of him, stuck in a visual loop. I was remembering, not seeing, Wyatt.

At three o'clock, according to the alarm clock on the bedside table, I reached over to touch my son's body through the covers. He roused, shaking the hand off, muttering and smacking his lips, curling closer into himself. The relief was almost overwhelming.

"Are you sick, Wyatt?" I asked. "Do you feel okay? Can I get you something?"

Each of my actions felt oddly familiar but also ill-fitting, as if I were putting on the mask and mien of a mother. "Can I get you anything," I asked. An odor rose from under the disarranged covers, the pungency of a boy's body mixed with something both sweet and rotten, not like the stench of death but something else. I sat for a long time trying to place the odor. It smelled natural, rich and verdant, as if there were things growing inside the darkness around his body. Fungal or vegetable growth.

When my ringtone sounded, a song from my childhood, I scurried out of the room and answered the call with a hurried "what"; my mother saying, "Did you eat today yet?" Her voice had holes in it I could fall down inside.

"No."

"Eat," she said. "Eat, Danielle."

"I have to go," I said. "I will. I'll eat."

Wyatt's presence pulled at me as I walked down the stairs. It took a great effort to pull myself away from him. It felt like betrayal, every second away from him a wasted opportunity.

I took the pineapple my mother had brought me the day before out of the fridge, sliced it in half, the yellow slick and sticky and bright, cutting around the hairy spikes and the core, taking the sweet acid into my mouth. I stood sucking the pieces of pineapple into pulp then spitting the pulp out, as if even eating had become unfamiliar to me. I kept telling myself that Wyatt was upstairs. In bed. That he had returned. Hope and joy threatened to breach the wall of my indifference, a wall I had built stone by stone over the past month, the woman inside me hauling them up from the deepest depths and carefully arranging them, ensuring that there were no chinks between them. It had been the hardest work of my life.

I was still standing in the kitchen when Wyatt walked through the room and out the sliding glass doors onto the back deck. He wore a red t-shirt and black jeans with frayed cuffs. His feet were bare, the condition of his feet abysmal, as if he had walked miles without wearing shoes. I imagined him walking up out of a cave, through a meadow, across dirt roads. He did not look at me but walked outside as if on a mission. Then he stood in the center of the back deck, his face angled toward the sun. He looked unspeakably beautiful, the sun highlighting his light eyebrows and shining through his ears. He looked like a boy who'd just woken up, still half in the world of dreams, still loaded full of fantastic images.

I texted my mother, assuring her that I had eaten, put the pineapple back in the fridge, then joined my son on the back deck.

Wyatt remained unmoving in the sun until evening, and then he walked through the house and upstairs, back into his room. He sat at his desk, a small simple black desk he'd picked out at Ikea. He turned on his tablet and watched cartoons, his eyes still. It was as if the images from the tablet were flowing into his eyes, feeding something behind them. I watched for a long time before, finally, I went into my bedroom, undressed, and climbed under the covers. Stephan called from Barcelona and asked how I was doing, a quick, stilted conversation. If Stephan could somehow teleport back to our home, could hold me against him, or if I could hold him, if we could find some kind of even mild relief in each other. It was hard for me to even picture him as he spoke.

I truly slept for the first time in a month. When I woke I was sure he would be gone, but there he was in his bed, in the same position he'd been in the morning before.

HIS SCHEDULE WAS NOT MY SCHEDULE. He would sleep through the days and, if I did not disturb him, wake at around four p.m., when he would make his way out to the deck to stand in the sun, a battery in need of recharging. Most mornings, I would sit by his bedside, watching him. He was always in the same position, face turned away from the room, his stick-out ears and the nape of his neck facing me. I could smell the odor of him from before—or I told myself I could smell him through the new odor of rot and growth. I'd had no idea how much those two things smelled alike.

I wanted, desperately, to shuck the red t-shirt from his body and put it in the wash. I wanted him to wear clean clothes. I wanted to bathe him, to wash tenderly around the bruises I assumed were there, the purple yellowing. But I could not bring myself to touch him, except through the thick covers on the bed, and then only tentatively, for a second.

My mother arrived on the second day of Wyatt's return, bearing a lima bean casserole. She poured lemonades. We sat out on the deck. She searched my face, and I tried to smile. I picked at clotted cheese in the casserole, ate what I could. My mother nattered away, telling me about a book she thought I might like. Was I reading anything? I shook my head.

When Wyatt walked onto the deck and angled his face toward the sun, I watched my mother, waiting for her reaction. She didn't see him. For her, he was not there. His eyebrows and hair were turning lighter. He'd been fair as a toddler, but his hair had darkened over the years. Now he was becoming fair again. He always did, in the summer, but not like this. His ears were translucent. I was afraid he was going to fade out, but I couldn't express that fear. My mother looked at me looking at Wyatt, concern stamped on her face.

"I'm okay," I said, trying to smile. Strangely, I was relieved she couldn't see him—though that fact also made me feel like I was falling down an endless dark tunnel.

"Do you want me to stay the night? I'm worried about you being alone like this."

"No. Jenn is coming tonight," I lied. "I'll be fine. And I have support group tomorrow."

AFTER WYATT RETURNED, it became easier to remember him, to recall specific details, as if his physical presence allowed the memories to take on the weight of lived experience. He had loved—he did love?—insects, the more bizarre the better, collected pictures of them, had hundreds of images saved on his tablet, drew them with hairy legs and compound eyes, theorized new insects in new environments, dreamed about discovering new species when he got older. He was gifted and odd, odder than I'd been as a child. He taught me about the boundaries of what was normal and how sometimes crossing those boundaries was necessary. Sometimes, even when he was alive, I felt distant from him. I pretended to be interested in the bugs he showed me. I wanted to see the world as he did. I wanted to spare him, to the degree I could, from the expectations of society, what it meant to be a boy, what it would mean to be a man.

It was absurd that he had died so young. Every mother fears it, no mother is ever prepared for it. No mother ever can be. Even mothers with advance warning, mothers whose children suffer incurable diseases, are blindsided by it. It is the most overwhelming experience.

I wanted to sleep on the floor of his bedroom, curled up, but didn't dare. I would hear the tablet all night. The same cartoons, over and over again. Antic animals with plastic human faces. Sometimes I'd hear him walking down the stairs at four a.m. and I would wonder what he was doing down there.

I allowed him free rein.

ALL MY CLOTHES HAD BECOME too big for me. I was dwindling. I pulled on a summer dress I'd worn in my twenties but swam even in that. I slid into sandals and stood at the front door for a long time, my hand on the doorknob. I didn't want to leave while Wyatt was in the house. He would be sleeping for several more hours, but leaving him felt wrong.

While I walked down the front steps and got into the car, I felt like I was betraying him. I felt ashamed. But I also felt like if I didn't leave I would waste away inside the house, that I might also die. Maybe I already had. The sun was intense, but I didn't wear sunglasses. By the time I got to the old elementary school, blobs of bright colors danced behind my eyes.

It was a strange act of cruelty to hold these support group meetings at the former elementary school, a gothic structure converted into a community center. The marble stairs were chipped, the brick face imposing, the foyer echoing. Many people came only to use the pool, and there was the pervasive chlorine smell that always made me think of purgatory, older people in flip flops waddling down the hallways. The younger people went to their swim clubs in the summer. I thought of Wyatt and his slim, bare chest, the way he would jump off the side of the pool, heedless of anyone below. He'd been heedless of so much. I regret that I was not there when it happened, when the car impacted him, but I am relieved I did not hear it, the way Stephan did, that I don't have to carry that sound for the rest of my life. I carry only the imagined sound. The squeal of tires. The impact. The driver's side door slamming shut. The woman who killed him holding her hand before her mouth, trying to stop something, her soul?, from escaping.

There were only three others at the meeting. Usually there were seven or eight, mostly mothers, a few fathers. Only mothers on this day, one of them Janice Grossman, the facilitator of the group, a woman with a slash for a mouth and a deep voice. She led us in meditation. It was impossible to clear the mind even on the best days, but after what I had been through…. It was stupid to even try. Janice's voice was deep, intoning, telling us to let go of all negative energy, to let out the darkness and let in the light. I wanted to smash her head like a watermelon. I wanted to choke her fleshy neck. I felt ashamed of but not accountable for these feelings.

The meeting was more awkward than usual, no one willing to say more than a few words. We sat in an old classroom squeezed into chairs designed for children the age of our dead children. I looked at the faces of the mothers and knew none of them were going through what I was going through. For them, their children were simply gone. I felt guilty for my good fortune. Then I couldn't believe I thought of it as good fortune.

Breanna and I dawdled in the room after the others left. "Do you want to get a coffee?" she asked. I nodded, even though what I wanted to do was go back to Wyatt. My heart was directing me home, but my feet turned left on the sidewalk. We went to Beans in the Belfry and ordered two coffees.

We sat by the window and stared at cars passing on Main Street. Neither of us could talk. We had things to say but they were too big; they nested just below our tongues.

Then Breanna leaned forward and said, "He's back." Her face was deeply lined, the skull underneath it plain, but you could tell she had once been the most beautiful girl in whatever high school she went to. She had not had to deal with adversity until her son died—drowning during a family trip to the Eastern Shore. It had been like a plank smacking her in the face.

I acted like I didn't know what she was talking about.

"What do you mean?"

"Jonathan. He's back. He sleeps a lot, but he's back." She looked out the window. "You probably think I'm crazy." I imagined her boy with seaweed draping his thin shoulders.

"Wyatt is back, too," I said.

We stared at each other the way two crazy people caught in the same delusion stare at each other. I wondered if the others who had missed the meeting were with their dead children. Maybe they had *all* returned. Maybe all children return and we never knew it because we were not in the sad sorority of childless mothers.

There was not much we could say to each other.

When she left, Breanna smiled a strange smile, the same smile I felt on my face.

DAYS PASSED. STEPHAN'S RETURN became imminent. He called every day, and we marshalled words and sent them across the air toward each other. After every support group meeting Breanna and I would sit at the coffee shop and exchange a few words about our sons. "He's still back," we would say.

I asked Breanna if her son smelled different and she nodded in a knowing way. "I can't place it," she said.

Wyatt became lighter and lighter, but at the same time he seemed to stabilize. He was not fading. His hair was tow-headed, his eyes pale blue. I drank afternoon tea on the deck. Days were getting shorter.

I started to talk to him, to tell him how much I missed him, how much I loved him and always would. I talked about what he would have become. A scientist. An artist. Something out of the ordinary. I told him how grateful I was that he was back. I dreaded Stephan's return. When we talked on the phone, I could tell he was getting drunk with colleagues. Maybe he was having an affair. I didn't care.

The day before he was to arrive, I awoke to darkness, an overcast sky. My dreams had been murky and strange, but they dissolved the second I woke. It was later than usual, nearly ten o'clock. I sat in the living room with a coffee trying to read a novel my mother had recommended. The words did not string themselves together in a sensible way.

Wyatt came down the stairs at three o'clock. He stopped before the sliding glass doors. For the first time, I sensed some sentience inside him. He paused and there was a ripple of movement around his eyes, the muscles pulling taut. Rain coursed across the glass.

"It's okay, Wyatt," I said.

I still don't know why I said it, or what I meant when I said it. "It's okay," I said. I didn't want to say those words, but I had to. That is the way of all mothers. I was a lost mother in a world of lost mothers. I was not special in any way. I did not deserve any of this.

Wyatt opened the door and walked out into the rain.

Mystery Hill

Allan weighed 532 pounds, and he lived in the attic of the house on Mystery Hill. Downstairs was the gift shop and the "museum," which contained artifacts found on the site when it was excavated in the 1970s. Prehistoric "tools" that looked like regular rocks inside plexiglass cases. A set of manacles and an old pair of half-disintegrated eyeglass frames. Behind the museum and gift shop was a section where his mother and her boyfriend, Fred, lived, with a kitchen, TV room, bedroom and bathroom. His mother made him food and carried it up to him, large plates of pasta and meat and potatoes, comfort food. It had been years, it was hard to remember exactly how long, since Allan had been able to negotiate the stairs and walk outside.

When his mother first met Fred and they'd moved into the house on Mystery Hill with him, Allan had taken care of the alpacas, which Fred had added as an attraction for people not attracted by the mystery. Even then Allan had been large, and he had never liked taking care of the alpacas. They spit at him and looked at him suspiciously, in a way that creeped him out, so Fred hired a girl who wanted to be a veterinarian but wound up working at Mystery Hill instead. Her name was Casie. Maybe because she was the only girl he saw regularly, Allan was in love with her and had been for years.

He would watch her work from an easy chair drawn up beside the window. Casie wore flannel shirts, jeans, and duck boots. Different shirts and jeans, but always the same boots. He would watch her ferrying food to the sheds for the alpacas in an old wheelbarrow, sometimes hay, more often random branches. The alpacas didn't need all that much attention, so Casie also did other things around the place. She maintained the trails, worked the register when Fred or Allan's mother were not around, gave tours occasionally. She had a splotchy birthmark on her neck and her nose had been flattened at one time and not set back right, and Allan knew that other people would not find her particularly attractive, but that made her doubly attractive to him. It was like only he could see through her average appearance to her true beauty. Casie knew Allan was up there—they'd met and talked about normal everyday things, like the weather, when she was first hired—and sometimes she would look up toward the window, smile and wave at him, but she never made any move to walk up the stairs to talk to him. He wondered what they told her about him. He wondered what she thought about him.

From the window, beyond the alpaca enclosure, Allan could see the excavated rock formations that made the hill a mystery. Some people, mostly Fred, took the site ultra-seriously. Fred truly believed prehistoric men had constructed the site, that they'd arranged the rocks in such a way that the sun and moon interacted with the rocks in a specific manner during solstices and equinoxes, etc. Fred also believed that what they called the "sacrificial table," a flat slab of a rock with runnels carved into its sides, had, in fact, been precisely that, a sacrificial table, that virgins had been sacrificed here while prehistoric men pretending to be oracles hid under the speaking tube, chanting.

Most other people who visited the site were not nearly so convinced, taking it in stride, in good humor, as a kind of joke. It was just a jumble of random rocks and part of an old foundation wall to them. Most visitors came from far away or stumbled onto the site in some guidebook of oddities.

Allan had been thirteen, living in a normal suburban neighborhood full of identical ranch houses, when he first heard about Mystery Hill. Everyone in town knew about it, though not many had ever visited it. This had been during the heyday of the "Satanic Panic," when the entire country had been gripped by the fear that teenagers, thanks to Ozzy Osbourne and Dungeons & Dragons, were becoming Satanists en masse, and Mystery Hill was supposedly the locus of Satanic activity in the town, where they congregated to do their dark deeds, perform their occult rites or whatever. When he was a teenager, back before he became morbidly obese, during a brief period when he had friends, Allan had climbed the fence with a bunch of other wastoids, foisting his flab over the top of the fence with difficulty. They explored the site, high as hell. It felt eerie as they ran around the hill at night, poking their heads into chambers and talking through the "speaking tube." He'd never admitted to anyone quite how freaked out he'd been that night, how he'd imagined hoary Satanic figures coming out of the woods to drag them into the shadows and chop them into little pieces, and he never would have expected that he would live here someday. Now little cameras that Fred monitored were strapped to the trees, and hardly anyone tried to break in anymore.

Every new year, following the winter solstice, which Fred made a huge deal out of, inviting photographers to catch the last light of the sun as it aligned with the so-called "solstice monolith," Allan would make a resolution. He would tell himself that *this* would be the year he went on a diet and stuck with it. This would be the year he would lose weight, come down from the attic, and make his reappearance in the world. This would be the Year of Allan. He had secret plans about what he would say to Casie once he saw her face-to-face, plans he barely told himself.

Following his resolution, he would leave the plates of over-heaping food untouched on the table, would throw it all into the trash bags his mother left for him once it went cold. He would refuse all sustenance, his insides grumbling and groaning like prehistoric man. He would struggle and suffer, enduring massive headaches and becoming horribly mean-tempered. What did it matter if he was mean-tempered? He only ever interacted with his mother anyway, and even their interactions were brief, in the winter.

During most of the year his mother would come up to the attic room, which was still decorated as it had been when he was eighteen, with posters of fantasy art by H.R. Giger and Frank Frazetta, sit at the table, and tell him news of the world, and, more pointedly, of the small town. He could watch the TV and find out the news of the world if he wanted to, and he *did* follow the big elections, the acrimony in the country deepening, the wars that never seemed to end, the hatred toward certain groups of people that kept coming back around. But it all seemed so distant from him. He didn't really care. He cared even less about the old high school classmates his mother told him about, listing off their accomplishments or their tragedies. One of them had killed himself, a gunshot to the temple. Another had been arrested for child pornography. And the other had become the governor of the small state. She told him about the friends she had lunch or coffee with when she left Mystery Hill, Judy and Gladys and Tanya, women like her who had found a way to pass their entire lives in the small town. They had health issues and family problems. They endured hysterectomies and divorces. Their children got rheumatoid arthritis. Their children gave birth to grandchildren with holes in their hearts. Some of them won awards or went off to North Carolina to live off the grid. Allan was forced to listen to it all, but during the winters, especially when he was dieting, his mother would simply place the food on his table and hie away.

He looked out the window at the cold rain falling on the hill. The trees dripped. Casie walked the grounds with her green raincoat hood covering her head.

No one came to the hill for several days in a row. The rain turned to snow, but it was an ugly snow.

Then a bobcat got into the alpaca enclosure and killed one of the alpacas. Allan felt bad watching Casie drag the body out from the enclosure, wished he could help, or at least be there for her. He was sure she had names for each of the alpacas. He was pretty sure this was the first of the animals that had died since they first arrived in crates from South America. The alpaca's stomach had been torn open by the sharp little teeth of the bobcat and its insides ballooned out. It was strangely frightening. He watched Casie load the body onto the bed of a small trailer and drive it off down the trail using the four-wheeler she drove everywhere. She was probably going to bury it. He wished he could be down there with her, could help dig the grave, could comfort her. It was a missed opportunity.

She repaired the fencing where the bobcat got in and stroked the necks of the panicked alpacas that remained.

Meanwhile Allan felt his body eating itself. Eventually he knew he would give in and start eating again, that he could not go on like this much longer. His motivation was not strong enough. Eventually he would go back to his old ways. This is how it went every year: he would last a few days before finally giving in and going back to eating the way he always had, shoving it all in. His mother acted like nothing was happening, didn't question him, simply delivered the food and left. That had always been her way, even back when it was just the two of them alone. She'd always pretended that everything was fine, as if pretending could make it so. It had never brought his father back or stopped the bullying. His father had left his mother for Nevada and another woman, and he had left Allan because he was fundamentally unlovable.

Allan was not sure exactly how old he was, because he had stopped celebrating birthdays, but he was probably in his early thirties. Casie was also getting older. Her hair was no longer as lustrous as it had been. She wore a dark green winter hat that was new this year. She was filling out. Then Allan realized that she was filling out because she was pregnant.

At first he felt affronted, as if she'd done something behind his back. He had never really thought about Casie's life outside of Mystery Hill before. He knew she existed outside of Mystery Hill, of course, but it was like she disappeared over the horizon when she left in the early evenings, and he could no longer even think about her. She went over the event horizon. As he watched her walking out to the alpaca enclosure, he imagined a fetal alpaca curled inside her belly. Strangely, the alpaca fetus had his face.

He felt a mixture of sadness and anger, more powerful emotions than he'd felt in years. He grew dizzy from hunger but refused to give in. Days passed. He watched the television and read the books his mother brought him from the library. He would read anything, but his favorite author was Piers Anthony. He loved the *Incarnations of Immortality* series. He liked anything that transported him to another place. He guessed that he had lost eight to ten pounds already. He still couldn't get out of the bed or the easy chair without great difficulty, did so only once or twice a day to perform his ablutions, as he thought of them. Defecating, washing up. Since he wasn't eating, he didn't need to get up nearly as often as before. He raised his arms in a pantomime of exercise, twisted his huge girth from side to side. He felt monstrous. He had not always been a monster, and there was a person inside him waiting to get out. If it wasn't too late.

He watched Casie, the way he always had, as she fed the alpacas and maintained the trails. Even pregnant she was robust, swinging an ax, breaking up branches, operating the chipper. He admired her forthrightness, her determination, her strength. He wondered who the father was, but only briefly.

His mother came up to the attic and cleared away the food he hadn't eaten.

"I'm getting worried about you, Allan," she said, sitting down at the kitchen table he never used. "You haven't eaten in days. That's no way to lose weight. That's not good for you."

"It seems to be working," he said, lifting a flap of empty skin.

"But it's not healthy, honey."

He shrugged, looked out the window. He loved his mother and appreciated her concern, but he was his own person. The day was ugly, again, but Casie existed inside it like a bright spot of red flannel. She wore her new green cap.

"Is she married now?"

"Who?"

"Casie."

"Oh… I have no idea." She seemed taken aback by his curiosity. "Why? You really need to eat something, Allan. I can make something healthy, if that's what you really want. I can make you a salad."

"Ha!"

When he looked at his mother now, he saw a middle aged woman. She had not been middle aged before. She'd been young and vibrant when they first moved here. So full of life. Happy with her new relationship, after so long alone. Excited to be living in a new place. At least she'd acted that way around Allan. They'd decorated his new attic space together, painted the walls, put up the posters, moved in the bed and the bookcase. His own place. He'd been a teenager then, but he had let her act like she was taking care of him.

Because that was what she needed. Now it was like the hill had sapped her youth away, like it was killing her. Maybe *that* was the mystery of Mystery Hill. Maybe it killed its keepers. He felt stupid. There was no mystery. There had never been any mystery.

He ate a few spoonfuls of mashed potatoes for her sake. They melted in his mouth and made blood course through his veins, and he had to stop himself from shoving the rest of the heaping pile in after them. After she left he dumped the rest in the trash bag and left the bag by the stairs.

His mother did not come back.

Days passed.

The snow built up outside. A foot, then two feet, then two and a half feet. Casie shoveled a path between the museum and the alpaca enclosure. No visitors arrived. The sunsets had become achingly beautiful, as if the world were on fire. Allan opened the trash bag, but the mashed potatoes had all gone bad and were starting to stink. He went to the door and called down for his mother. He was hungrier than he could remember ever being. He could eat a cow.

"Maaa," he shouted. He felt dumb. He was a thirty-something year old man yelling for his mommy. "Maaa," he shouted.

No sound came from the dark downstairs. He could almost fit through the doorway now, but not quite. He wondered if Fred had murdered his mother. Maybe Fred was the father of the alpaca baby inside Casie's stomach. Maybe he was living inside some sordid soap opera. Or a horror movie. Maybe the Satanic Panic had become real, and his mother had been sacrificed. But no, he refused to believe any of that. There had to be a logical explanation for everything.

Finally, Fred made his way slowly up the stairs. He carried a small plate of au gratin potatoes and overlapping slices of spiral ham. He wore a dark suit and tie and looked beaten down, his shoulders sagging. It'd been years since Allan had seen the man, and he looked different now. The Fred in his memory was not this Fred. His face used to look like an arrowhead—at least it did to younger Allan. Now it looked droopy, one eye lower than the other. His curly hair had turned white at the temples. He looked like the kind of man who believed in aliens and Bigfoot.

"I am so sorry, Allan," he said, as if Allan was supposed to know what he was talking about, as if they were continuing a conversation they'd already started.

"What are you sorry about?" Allan said. His voice sounded different to his ears, softer, more tremulous.

"Your mother."

And then Fred was sitting at the table sobbing. Allan got up from the bed. It took a great effort, but a little less effort than before. He'd lost twenty or thirty pounds. If he could lose that much, he knew he could lose much more. He was torn between comforting this man he barely knew and didn't like all that much, and falling onto the food. Food won. He scarfed down the ham and potatoes as Fred sobbed.

In the beginning, Fred had made it perfectly clear that he was never going to be Allan's stepfather, only his mother's boyfriend, and when Allan didn't show any enthusiasm for the minute details of the excavations Fred tried to share with him, their separate ways were sealed.

Now they settled into a kind of truce. Fred brought him food every day, normal portions, not the heaping portions his mother used to bring. Sometimes there was fruit. An apple or a pack of blueberries. Allan felt hungry all the time, and angry, and sad, because his mother had passed away suddenly in the night of an aneurysm, but he also felt healthier than he had in years. He watched Casie wandering the trails of Mystery Hill, always doing something practical, fencing in the old well, straightening a stone wall, or putting up new directional signs. Small groups of visitors arrived, walking out to the rock formations through the melting snow. Some of them laughed and some of them took it seriously, kneeling down in the chambers to inspect "pictographs" that were probably just random shapes in the rocks.

Sometimes, still, it felt magical to Allan, living on Mystery Hill. Sometimes he could feel the history of the place seeping up all around him. He wasn't convinced that anything supernatural had ever happened here, didn't think the sacrificial table was actually a sacrificial table, but things had definitely happened here in the past. Runaway slaves had been hidden here, for sure. There *were* kids who'd done Satanic rituals here back in the 80s. There was a kind of magic here, somehow. He'd felt it from the beginning, when they first moved in. At first, having survived the psychological gauntlet that was high school, he had just liked to spend time alone in his new space, reading, watching TV, daydreaming. His mother came up with his food every day, but at that time she didn't spend long talking to him. Then he realized he'd been up there for three years and he looked down on himself and realized he couldn't fit out the door. He didn't really care, at first.

He spent a lot of his time indulging in fantasies he would never share with anyone, fantasies too embarrassing for the real world, fantasies in which he was the hero or an elf or a supernatural creature of some kind, with intense powers. He built his own worlds.

Casie's stomach grew. Winter turned to spring. Finally, Allan found that he could fit down the stairs for the first time in years. At first he resisted the urge. He walked in circles in the attic for exercise, looking over at the door now and then. He psyched himself up.

One day when the sun was melting the layer of snow, and thick icicles were barring his view out the window, he finally did it; he walked downstairs. The dim stairway was even narrower than he remembered, with a corner that took some negotiating. The museum and the gift shop were exactly as they had been before. The same "tools" and "artifacts" were inside plexiglass cases, the same t-shirts and mugs were on display, and there were the same bins of smooth rocks that kids could collect inside little drawstring bags. Three women speaking German were looking at geodes. A tall man with sparse hair looked at the world map of monoliths, each site featured in a blurry photograph, yarn pinned to the exact locations. A couple was watching the informational film about Mystery Hill in the small dark side-room, the same film that had played years before, featuring an archeologist with wispy gray hair and a skeletal head explaining the arti-facts. It was all so strange. Everything was exactly as it had been when he went up into the attic. Nothing had changed, except Fred had aged, Casie was pregnant, and his mother was dead.

Fred blinked at him from behind the cash register. Allan waited for someone else to notice him, for the mockery to begin, but no one looked at him twice.

He moved the way a young colt moves, unsure on his feet. He had to catch his breath every few steps. Outside, Casie was leaning against the wire fence of the enclosure looking in at the alpacas. Allan was bad with animals, but he was pretty sure there were more of them now than there had been before. One of them appeared to be a youngster, its body smaller and less heavily furred than the others. They all turned their weird faces in his direction to look at him. Maybe that was just the way they looked, maybe they didn't dislike him in particular.

"Hey," Casie said, as if she weren't surprised to see him down from the attic, as if it were perfectly natural for him to be there.

"Hey," he said back.

"I'm sorry about your mother."

He nodded.

The two of them, mother and son, had been all the other had for a long time, until she met Fred. The neighborhood full of ranchers had been near the woods, and when he was a kid he would go out into them, exploring. Sometimes his mother would join him, hiking out to the pond in the middle of the woods, where they would eat lunch and laugh. She had given him advice about girls and school, where he should go to college, all that. She'd pretended like he wasn't being bullied—the usual; mockery and physical abuse, his girth slammed into lockers, his head pressed against one of the tall porcelain urinals. They'd watched black and white movies together at night, a practice that ended definitively after she met Fred. He had hated her sometimes, but more often he felt an overwhelming love for her. It had taken him years to forgive her for moving in with Fred. He realized that he barely knew anything about her.

He'd been pretty smart back when he was younger. Anything had seemed possible. It was hard to believe he'd spent so long in an attic by himself, in self-exile. He thought maybe it wasn't too late to go back to school, figure out something to do. He had no idea how to do the most normal things in life, how to buy food or get an apartment or apply for jobs, but it couldn't be that hard.

"Congratulations," he said. He could hear the sadness in his own voice. This was not what he had been planning to say to her.

Casie turned to look at him. She smiled and instinctively touched her bulging belly. He still imagined it as an alpaca, a bigger alpaca baby with his own face, but he knew it was a human baby inside there with someone else's face, and that it was lucky to have Casie as its mother.

"Thanks, Allan. It's good to see you."

"It's good to see you too. I'll talk to you later," he said.

He made his way out to the rock formations. He went through the chambers, bending down to look at the pictographs, breathing heavily. Then he stood at the summit of the hill and looked off toward where the sun was setting. All the monoliths poked out of the snow, and it *did* look like someone at some time had moved them into place. Everything seemed so perfectly arranged.

Acknowledgments

Gratefully acknowledged are the following publications, where stories appeared in earlier versions:

"If I Ran My Hand Over Your Head, I Would Bleed" appeared in *Digital Americana Magazine*

"Kavita" appeared in *CutBank*

"Whippet" appeared in *Adirondack Review*

"Beasts" appeared in *Manila Envelope*

"Cold Cold Bright Bright" appeared in *Northwind Magazine*

"Leaving Indian Summer" appeared in *Bayou Magazine*

"Mousekiller" appeared in *Switchback*

"Dogs" appeared in *Flash Fiction Magazine*

"Lost Mothers" appeared in *Invisible Cities*

"A Wolf at the Door" appeared in *The Dodge*

"American Animism" appeared in *Willows Wept Review*

"Our Lady of Eternal Sorrows" appeared in *Marrow Magazine*

"K9" appeared in *Punk Noir*

"The Blue of Broken Bones" appeared in *Quarter After Eight*

Thanks to: my kids, Evangeline and Alex; my mother Maureen and father Dan; my brother Chris; my ex-wife Karry Albert Gallagher; my friends forever Chris Battles, Paul Baylis, Mark Webster, Ross DeHarpporte, and Erin Battles; mentors and teachers Andre Dubus III, Ann Green, J.C. Hallman, Jo Parker, April Lindner, Tom Coyne; fellow writers, Anne Vukicevich, Melanie Kuchma, Ted Fristrom, Sam Kimball, Kim Jensen, and Dave Truscello.

Thanks to everyone at Cornerstone Press, including editorial director Brett Hill, editorial assistants Cora Bender and Lillian Kulbeck, managing editors Kylie Newton and Eva Nielsen, senior editor Ellie Atkinson, media director Ava Willett, sales director Sophie McPherson, and publisher Dr. Ross Tangedal.